MATT ZURBO is a bush worker in the Otway Ranges in Victoria.
He is madly jealous of anyone who can sing or play a
musical instrument.

Matt is the author of two young adult novels, *Idiot Pride*, which
was shortlisted for the 1998 CBC Book of the Year Awards, and
Flyboy and the Invisible, and two picture books, *Blow Kid, Blow*,
illustrated by Jeff Raglus, and *I Got a Rocket*, illustrated
by Dean Gorrisen.

HOT NIGHTS COOL DRAGONS

MATT ZURBO

CPL YA

ALLEN&UNWIN

The author would like to acknowledge Abbott and Costello
for their Ham Sandwich routine.

First published in 2004

Allen & Unwin
83 Alexander Street,
Crows Nest NSW 2065 Australia
Phone: (61 2) 8425 0100
Fax: (61 2) 9906 2218
E-mail: info@allenandunwin.com
Web: www.allenandunwin.com

National Library of Australia
Cataloguing-in-Publication entry:
Zurbo, Matt, 1967– .
Hot nights cool dragons.
ISBN 1 74114 178 8.
1. Title.
A823.3

Cover and text design by ...oid design
Part title images by Rupert Gibb
Set in 12/17 pt Matrix Regular by Midland Typesetters
Printed in Australia by Griffin Press

10 9 8 7 6 5 4 3 2 1

Dedicated to

Music and driving

The Monaros
Bookings and CDs Phone (03) 55 625 650

Sassy's music: Tony Gould, Virus, Theolonius Monk, Fogg,
12 Tone Diamonds, Jamie Oehlers. *Bobby's music:* The Exotics,
The Sonics, The Mummies, Mr Floppy, The Hard Ons, The Dirtbombs,
The Cosmic Psychos, Scott Walker. *John Piero's music:* Chris Wilson
and Sarah Carroll, The Spoils, Captain Beefheart.

And the band playing at your pub this Saturday night.

1. Heat

The nights were hot that summer. As hot as red coals. The air was still as a sunken ship. The whole city tossing and turning, bad tempered, trying to get to sleep.

Bobby lay awake listening to music. Live jazz climbed the walls of his flats, drifting through his open window, from somewhere within the shadows and moonglow of the streets.

Bobby hated jazz, but, man, to hear it lost out there in the night made him feel like he was taking an ice-bath. Jazz seemed to sound better when the air was fire-hot.

He made his way into Sassy's room. Shook her bed with his foot.

'C'm'ere,' he hissed to his sister. 'Listen.'

Sassy rubbed her eyes, yawned. Made her way out from sleep.

'Can you hear it?' he said, dragging her towards his window.

He was older than her, but so what. They had a bond, a rule: *Never leave the other behind*. Still, she was tired, half-awake, sticky with sweat.

'Hear what? Who cares?'

'Listen —' Bobby gave her another push.

The moon was out in all its glory. The street a million quiet shades of silver and neon glow.

Sassy said nothing for a long while. Her ears strained, scouting the midnight, catching up to where Bobby's had been.

1

'What?'

'Listen!' Bobby said.

'. . . Jazz?'

'Yeah. Let's go.'

'What? Out there?'

'Sure. I can't sleep. It's something to do.'

Bobby and Sassy climbed down the fire-escape, listened for the jazz, then followed its flow.

It was even hotter down below, the air so still and thick, black cats had to swim through it. A few people shuffled up and down the footpath in cotton dressing-gowns, floppy t-shirts and dirty tracky-daks. In things you throw on when your brain is melting and you just can't sleep.

Bobby and Sassy avoided them, and the policemen, and the One Man Carnival, selling tickets out front of the all-night cinema. Sweat ran down his chubby, angled face, filling his collar, but he just kept sucking in hot air and shouting it out.

'COME ONE, COME ALL! ESCAPE THE HEAT! WE'VE GOT SOMETHING FOR EVERYONE . . .!' The One Man Carnival's voice echoed through the night, bouncing off buildings, assaulting stop signs and parking meters, before disappearing into one hundred open windows.

Brother and sister stood under a streetlight, listening for music. A fire truck screamed by, cutting through the night.

'It's the weather,' sighed Sassy. 'The whole city seems flammable.'

The fire truck worked its way around a far corner, like some big fat bolt of red flame, as though it was the truck, not the fire, that needed to be put out. People who had taken hours to get to sleep were suddenly awake and restless again.

Bobby and Sassy heard the sirens die, men shouting, activity. Smoke oozed through thick air. Water flowed along the gutter, back around the corner, towards them, before vanishing down the dusty, dry throat of a drain.

'Ssh!' hissed Bobby.

'I wasn't saying anything,' said Sassy.

'Sshh!' Bobby insisted. 'Listen.'

He pointed to a lane, its dark mouth surrounded by old brick walls. Drifting out from its forgotten reaches came the deep, slow sound of a lone trumpet.

Sassy could feel the streetlights sliding off her back as she and Bobby disappeared into the black tones of the lane.

'Maybe we should go home . . .' she said.

But Bobby didn't even hear her. He was locked on, following his ears further and further from home and all things safe . . .

Brother and sister waited for their eyes to adjust, listening to jazz unwind like something both friendly and sad.

Gradually, their eyes found their feet.

There was a factory on one side of the lane. It had thick, chicken-wire, green-glass windows, steam rising from its walls. The other side was a series of fire-escapes clinging desperately to tatty apartments. Halfway up the end ladder — wearing an old coal-miner's woollen hat, vest and slacks — a man played trumpet.

Bobby and Sassy looked through windows as they climbed to the nearest landing. Saw sleeping faces, lost in midnight ocean blues, despite the burning red of night.

Maybe the music is touching them, Sassy thought.

'Hey! Trumpet Man!' Bobby called.

'Sshh!' Sassy worried.

'Sshh!' a number of voices agreed.

Bobby and Sassy could just make out the shapes of people, hanging back in the shadows. There were two on the fire-escapes — one seemed to have a drum. A thin man with a clarinet sat on the wooden fence at the end of the lane. Even someone down at ground level holding a bass, leaning against a dumpster, right where they had walked.

Sassy wanted to say something. Anything. But had no words.

All the while the trumpeter sucked in smothering hot air and dark summer night. All the while he blew out cool, cool jazz.

As he finished his solo, the other people in the lane quietly tapped their instruments on railing, bins and bluestone. Bobby and Sassy could barely hear it, but in the silence it felt like a distant crowd. Applause.

Then one of the shapes on the fire-escape shifted, straightened. It was a beautiful black woman. She had strong shoulders and wore a glittering deep-green dress. Stepping out into moonglow, she began to sing. Not words, not that Bobby and Sassy could understand, no, she just . . . sang. Sang passionate, soulful sounds, as though she was easing the world.

The sleeping people swayed and sighed in their dreams. Bobby and Sassy lost all track of time, of space, of anything. They were so caught up, they didn't notice the trumpeter until he was right behind them, his lips hanging over their ears.

'You shouldn't be here,' he whispered. 'Blood boils when heatwaves get trapped in the moon. Crimes are committed, tempers flare . . .

'Snakes don't bother to go to sleep.'

Bobby stepped back, Sassy jumped and scrambled. The trumpeter's top half was still painted in shadow. It made his skin look warm grey. His goatee beard was ginger-red — the colour of rust, strength and good humour.

His face reminded Sassy of lazy days off spent swaying in a hammock.

His eyes carried stories.

'What's her name?' Sassy whispered.

4

The trumpeter looked at the woman of magic, her voice carrying all things midnight.

'Mona,' he smiled.

The trumpeter made his way to the roof. Bobby and Sassy followed. They watched Mona sing. Sometimes one or two of the other musicians joined in, playing around her, but never over her. Mostly they just listened as she rose in song.

Sassy had never felt anything like this. Not in all her thirteen years. She stood next to the trumpeter, watching with him, as Mona's music grew in passion, as it rose from the lane and into the murky sky.

Clouds were brewing.

'Why here?' asked Bobby.

Sassy noticed a ripple in the dark. A crack and a rumble from up in the hot, heavy sky. As though something was trying to break through.

Mona's voice grew stronger, reaching out from her soul.

The trumpeter leaned forward and Sassy saw the back of his neck. The skin was slightly lumpy, but smooth — like scales. She went to touch it, but he shifted to better watch the woman below.

'What are you people?' Bobby asked.

'We're dragons,' the trumpeter said, not taking his eyes off Mona.

'. . . Dragons?' Sassy stared at his skin, not sure what to believe.

'Wh . . . What do you call your band?' Bobby asked.

Like a tide flowing over rocks, Mona began to hit her peak.

Hearing Bobby's question, the trumpeter's grin rose. From side on Sassy could see a long sharp white tooth.

'What do we call our band?' he said. 'The Firebreakers.'

5

Just then, a loud crack shook the roof. The sky buckled. A cool breeze blew through a tear in the summer heatwave.

Sassy and Bobby looked up. First one drop fell, then two, then an avalanche of water tumbled down.

It fell all over their eyes and open, laughing mouths. The smell of wet dust and cooling cement rose from the ground. Relief and calm sighed throughout their world.

Down on the street the firemen cheered as though their never-ending war was over. The One Man Carnival ran for cover. People all over the city smiled, then drifted to sleep.

Bobby laughed and clapped and whooped as though life was a circus. A circus in the dark. And tonight, just tonight, he and his sister were its only audience.

Sassy didn't know up from down. She felt like the smallest thing.

Arms out, soaking up as much rain as possible, she walked to the edge of the building, desperate to hear more of Mona and her song. She looked down, but the lane was empty. The only sound she could hear was big, fat, juicy water-drops falling at her feet.

Even the trumpeter had gone.

It was as though the Firebreakers had brought rain with their music, then simply left.

Maybe they really were dragons, Sassy thought. *Descendants of them, or something.*

She could feel an incredible energy buzzing through her chest. She took in the moment, breathed deep, said nothing, didn't know what to think.

'Hot nights, cool dragons,' her brother chuckled beside her. 'I don't believe any of it.'

Bobby and Sassy walked home through the wet, midnight world, listening to a thousand drains gurgling like victory.

2. School

Months passed.

Winter fell on the city like a bad stuntman: with a heavy, spectacular, arms-flaying thud. Trees stripped naked to soak up the cold, necklines and kneecaps disappeared. The homeless fought each other just to stay warm.

Nothing really happened, though. Nothing changed.

There was no more mystery. Not for Sassy. No more Firebreakers, no midnight neon romance or strange rain.

'Johnny Apeshit? He's hot,' Maria said, as her cramped little radio pushed songs out over school lunchtime the way blankets cover dead animals.

'Yeah, hot,' agreed Jose.

'That boy who's just moved in? Why?' Sassy asked.

'God, *because*!' Julia moaned.

'Yeah, I mean, really . . .!' the others moaned, too.

Johnny Apeshit isn't hot, Sassy thought. *He's ordinary. They like him because he's too new to be old news yet. Because they haven't had a chance to mark him the way dogs pee all over light posts.*

They just like him because he's still a race. And they all want to beat each other to the line.

'What's your idea of hot, then, Sassy?' Jose demanded.

'Yeah,' Maria backed her up.

I met a person last summer who wasn't 'hot', but cooler than anything ever, Sassy wanted to tell them. *Who wore the night like a jacket, who played trumpet like a lazy moonrise.*

But what would her friends say to that? No, better to play it safe. 'What's hot?' Sassy said. 'I dunno.'

Maria's radio squeezed out more music. The song did its thing. As much as it was able.

She loves *him*, it told them, like all the other songs had told them. But *he* had better treat *her* right, it insisted.

Sassy's friends kept on agreeing with the song like chewing on gum. Like safe old news.

They agreed, even though they never told their boyfriends to treat them right. Even though they insisted on picking boyfriends who wouldn't treat them right. Not ever. They loved to complain about how their boys were like that. Loved to!

It beat doing something.

Another song had a go. It pushed out, through the screams and chatter of chilly school kids.

'I love this new tune!' Julie moaned.

Sassy listened.

He loves *her*, so it said. But *she* had better treat *him* right, it insisted.

All her friends loved it. Moaned with it. Because it was there. Because they needed something to spend their moans on.

'Have you seen the video clip? Her red jumpsuit?' Maria asked.

'Yeah.' Julie lit up. 'Does she thrust in it, or what?'

'What a tart!' Jose grumbled.

'She's a virgin.'

'Yeah, right!'

'No, really, she said!'

'Great! I hate blonde virgin tarts!' Jose wailed. 'I mean, sure she's confused, but why share it?'

Everybody laughed. Laughed easy. Except Sassy. She tried, but just couldn't. Her mind was racing. Racing hard.

Then the chorus re-emerged from two verses of padding. Sassy's friends moaned again.

Normally she'd moan, too. Would enjoy the tune, like her friends enjoyed it. But she had heard dragons! She'd listened to a song she didn't understand, in a moment too big for her, in a place too scary and brilliant to fully take in. A song that made her feel like her heart was being ripped out, gently, by gravity, dragged from her chest, into danger and romance.

She wanted to get these feelings out. Share them. But said nothing.

For some reason, like always, Sassy's friends stopped talking over the songs they loved and listened to five minutes of commercials.

Another song took a crack at it.

They think *each other* are pretty sexy, it said. And *they* will treat *each other* just right, *baby*!

'Dragons,' Sassy finally said.

Four or five months it had taken her, but here the topic was. Out in schoolyard air.

'What?' Maria asked.

'Dragons,' Sassy said. 'What if you saw something that seemed like dragons?'

Then this great, horrible barrage of obviousness rained down on her. Just like she knew it would. As sure as catching the flu on holidays.

'What drugs are you on?'

'Drag Queens?'

'Dragons? Get real! Me and Tahli Rockman once saw a UFO, though.'

'Who hasn't?'

'It's *true*! Well, she saw it more than me, but I was . . .'

'I don't know about UFOs, but a friend of a friend knows someone who swears she lived next door to that mass murderer. You know, the one on the telly? And he, so it goes, I swear, he was apparently a part of this cult thing where . . .'

'Your full of . . .'

'It's true . . .!'

'I saw a UFO, too . . .'

'So this friend picked up her phone, right? And there was this distant voice, right . . .?'

'You saw that on TV!'

'No really! I swear! She says . . .'

'She's right! I saw that show, too! You did see it on TV!'

'Did you read how that supermodel said her psychic told her . . .?'

One by one they filled in lunchtime, outdid each other with third-hand sightings of second-rate clichés. Shared comic-book tales.

But Sassy *had* seen. *Had* heard.

Had felt.

And this thing — these things, whatever they were — had given her an unbelievable hunger for more, then left. Never to return.

Sassy's hope and proof had come and gone. And she couldn't explain anything. There were just no words.

3. So Damn What

So what, Bobby thought. *So damn what.*

It had been months since that night. Since the Firebreakers. Winter was here. Autumn never happened. Summer had simply walked in front of a truck. Sassy was all broody. Now, that did bother him. Lots. But not at this moment.

Bobby had just found a dollar.

Found it down there, in the gutter outside the betting shop, lying on top of all those smoke butts and torn-up betting slips. Amongst all that losers' confetti.

A whole dollar, he thought.

'A dollar!' He shook it at the world.

Maybe he'd blow it on pinball, or a video game. A dim sim or potato cake. Then again he could crank up a thumping song on the pool-hall CD player. Get the whole miserable joint jumping. Give it a three-minute pulse, or something.

He flicked and rolled the dollar through his fingers. Walked along the footpath feeling fine, hamming up his fortune. Strutting like local Mafia, on top of it all.

The One Man Carnival was doing his thing outside the local cinema.

'WE SHOW 'EM AT 5! WE SHOW 'EM AT 7! AT 9 AND 11 . . .!' he bellowed at passers-by, at shop fronts, garbage bins and traffic lights.

'WE'VE GOT MONSTERS! DETECTIVES, MYSTERY! ROMANCE!
ESCAPE THE WORLD . . . !'

Bobby took a good look at him. Nobody was listening. Nobody
cared. Not even the One Man Carnival. He shouted to rattle your
teeth, to mess up your hair and bring down the world, but not once
did his face hold the slightest expression. Bobby thought about asking
the man to just shut up.

To shut up for a dollar.

Gradually, from somewhere beneath all that hard sell, Bobby
heard the slightest sound.

He stopped and listened, scratched at his ear lobe, poked at
its wax.

The noise, was it real? Yes. Just. It sounded like a drum. That
was it: the hollow, echoing rap of a snare drum, heard small, like a
mosquito teasing your dreams in the dead of night.

A snare drum. One stick. One steel brush for capturing the
drum's echo. To scrape cold, husky snake hisses back over the sharp
solid fact of an empty beat.

Rat-a tap tap, rat-a tap tap . . . it whispered, then hissed.

Rat-a tap tap! Rat-a tap tap!

Hisss!

The sound teased Bobby's view down a lane. In the daylight of
the next street, a man stood erect, busking.

He wore a faded, almost yellow, pinstripe suit, a pork-pie hat, the
drum around his waist. The man looked like a gangster, as though he came
from another time, before TV, when the world was a black-and-white,
scratchy movie. He had huge cheekbones, hollow cheeks, thin crab lips
shut tight by a hard jaw, stood too straight, too stiff. His face didn't move.

There was something mean about him. Bobby could feel it.

Rat-a tap tap. Rat-a tap tap.

Hisss.

Bobby watched the busker. The busker watched him. He slapped away, his beat filling the lane between them. Menace peeled off walls. Bad deeds found their feet.

Bobby knew things in that moment, without knowing how he knew them, or why.

He knew drums were the oldest instrument. Older than guitars, older than singing. Older than language. He knew drums could be made of sticks, that they could be made of bones. He knew they held a need for passion. A hunger for violence. In that moment he knew drums were as old as fire. That they were the sounds of battle, anger, war. That the sound of a drum was a collection of hits, knocks and punches.

He knew this drum wasn't just a drum. He could feel it.

The snare was pulling at Bobby, tugging his blood towards the lane, where hidden things grew with his sudden belief in hidden things.

The drum echoed. Its beat bounced off the walls, back onto itself, until its sound was like two drums, then four, then eight, sixteen, thirty-two, one hundred. Until the maths of it blurred. Drums raining everywhere.

Waves of drums. Tides of drums. The march of drums. Bass drums, tenor drums, voodoo drums.

The rhythm, the fury, of drums.

Bobby wanted to yell, yell anything to break up that damn beat.

'What do you want?' he shouted into the dark.

'Your dollar,' a voice whispered.

'Everything . . .' hissed another.

'Leave me alone!' Bobby yelled.

Then the man of snake sounds and hard reptile cheeks said something. He was over a block away, barely opened his hard, stretched mouth, yet his voice hissed, as though his was right there.

'You've got good ears . . .'

Bobby felt someone grab his shoulder, jerk him around. The cold winter's sun poured over his face.

'Hey, kid.'

And, with that, Bobby couldn't hear the drums. He couldn't hear anything anymore. Just traffic.

'I . . . I . . .' Bobby stammered. 'They want my dollar.'

'Listen . . .' the voice said. It was the One Man Carnival. He was looking past Bobby, down the lane.

He stared and stared, as if deciding things. His cheeks were round, his chin sharp, his nose big and hooked. Up close, he looked Middle Eastern, maybe Egyptian.

Finally he said, 'Be careful. Go home.'

Bobby turned.

The busker was gone and the menace that had filled the lane and given life to its shadows had left with him.

Bobby threw his dollar with spite at the lane, then bolted.

4. Dead Thing

John Piero was Sassy's father. He sat with his daughter in silence,
facing the TV. It cackled and squawked and promised them
everything — *credit cards accepted, conditions apply.* Sassy watched
without watching, listened without listening.

'Dad,' she finally said to the tube. 'I'm lost.'

'What's wrong, darling?' John Piero replied to the idiot box.

'I dunno,' Sassy told a hair commercial.

'Come on, honey. You can tell me,' her dad said, his pupils
bouncing in time with the lotto numbers.

Sassy had a slight shadow of the number 4 on her head. Then 33,
then 16. Then 2. Supplementary: 34.

Someone from somewhere in the flats yelled as though they had
broken their arm or maybe, just maybe, won something.

'I . . . I can't . . . explain . . . Did you win? The Lotto?'

'No. I told you, love: gambling is a mug's game. Money's too rare.
Let's stick to betting on each other . . .'

Then he faced her. John Piero was a short man, his face round,
head bald with black hair on its sides. Sassy loved him. It was that
simple.

'Come on . . . What's bothering you?'

'I . . . can't . . . I just can't . . .' Sassy's mouth tripped over itself.

By now the game show had fought its way back through the

15

commercials. The audience cheered on cue, because that's why they went to game shows — to do something with their day. To cheer, like they were told, before and after commercials.

'Is it school, honey?' John Piero asked.

Sassy shook her head.

The audience laughed.

'Is it boys? God, I hope not! I'm not ready for you and boys. I'll do a deal with you, honey. I'll give up smoking if you say you're not ready for boys . . .'

'It's not boys, Dad,' Sassy told the audience which was shouting: TAKE THE MONEY! TAKE THE MONEY!

'What is it, then?'

Tears rolled down Sassy's face, free and easy, while the audience booed and jeered some drongo who'd just blown half a million dollars because he didn't know which country Uluru was in.

Sassy's dad turned off the TV. Suddenly, it looked dead. Just plain dead. Now there were walls and things. There was a girl and a man. Sassy and her father.

'I can't find the words, Dad. I've . . . I've seen some . . . some *thing* I can't explain . . . and . . .' Sassy fell into a deafening silence.

Sassy's father thought about it. Or looked like he was. He always looked like he just might be thinking. As though he knew things, but wasn't smart enough to realise he knew them. Like they were bouncing around, in some big hollow part of his friendly round head, waiting for someone who was better at these things to rescue them.

'You've seen something you can't talk about?' he asked her.

She closed her eyes and nodded as though her head was her heart, her heart was her head and both were quietly, passionately agreeing with each other.

'Music,' she said. 'It's to do with music . . .'

That surprised him and worried him, for a thousand distant reasons. Music made the problem of boys seem easy.

It was at times like this he most missed Sassy's mother. But wishing never helped. She had died years ago. That's all there was to it.

He weighed things. The harder he thought, the more his brain hurt. In the end, he gave up on thinking and went with what he was best at. Caring. Let his heart do the talking.

'Honey, I'll be honest,' John Piero said. 'If . . . if you've found some kind of passion and it will hurt no one, I'm envious of you. Pursue it, chase it. Catch it, seize it.'

Sassy looked at him with doubt and flowing tears.

'But what if I don't . . . If I can't . . .? If I'm not . . .?'

Sassy's dad didn't know what she was talking about. He doubted she did. But her hunger seemed real enough. She was feeling, really feeling. And for him, that was enough to be glad.

'Sassy,' he said. 'Many people settle for things – a . . . a job, a partner, a house – simply because they don't know what they want to do. Not really. But . . . but direction . . . If you've found some . . . some kind of . . . hunger to give all that energy of yours focus, if some kind of hunger has found your heart . . . that is . . . I think you're the luckiest kid in the world.'

'But . . . It's so . . . I'm just a . . . How can I . . .?'

Sassy searched the room for help, as though the shelves and light bulbs might come running to her aid. Or the fridge might bound in from the kitchen, shouting all the right answers. But the room stayed square, still, quiet. There was just a couch, a dead TV and her dad, as bad at explaining himself as she was.

He meant well, but was all out of cleverness, his heart out of answers.

'Do what you've got to, baby,' he said. 'I'm here if you need me.'

Then he switched the TV on again. There was another commercial. One that he liked. He'd seen it maybe a hundred thousand times, but it still gave him a dull little smile, anyway.

5. Green Neon

There were new neon lights over the cinema. They burned the richest, deepest green. It seemed strange to Bobby, as if the street was a concrete hothouse, the footpath a hard, flat paddock, roamed by the occasional sly dog, shonky fat man, or shady woman.

Bobby had been watching, watching hard. Staring from the lane beneath his bedroom window. He could separate them: the visitors from the strangers, the tourists of the night from those who lived in it.

The buskers with their old lonely music, they belonged. The tired night cop, the bums. The waiter who did laps of the street, too shell-shocked from work to ever go home. The security guard who never guarded anything. Shades. All shades. Each one of them unapproved of by neighbours, parents and milk bar owners.

The not-quite-right people. All green. All neon.

And in amongst them was the One Man Carnival. Every centimetre, every hair, every drop of sweat on him was green, as if his bathtub at home might have neon rings around it. He was hot, loud air housed in a person, layering his voice over you like dust sticks to old photos.

Bobby wondered how he knew the busker with the snare drum – the Reptile. Just the thought of him made Bobby scared and angry. He wondered about the Reptile's connection to the

Firebreakers. First the jazz band, then the sleazy drummer. It was all connected. It had to be.

Somehow the One Man Carnival was a key. He was sure of it. Bobby watched the man.

He listened.

The One Man Carnival had ways. Rhythms. Sometimes he would shout in monotone. Other times he would bellow as though the only tool of his trade was capital letters. Tonight, every sentence he yelled had a word louder than the rest. That broke it all up and made you listen. That poke, poke, poked at you.

'Want to SEE a movie? We've got the LATEST movies! We've got OLD movies! We've got movies ABOUT movies! One day I'LL be in a movie! One day YOU'LL be in a movie! We ALL will! But . . . until then . . . COME IN AND SEE A MOVIE . . . !'

Blah, blah, blah, thought Bobby.

'YOU, sir! Yes, YOU! You THINK you don't want to watch a movie!' he roared at no one. 'But if you don't watch movies they won't MAKE movies! And if they don't MAKE movies, they can't pay the actor! And if they can't PAY the actor, the actor can't EMPLOY his housemaid! And if the housemaid has NO money, she won't be able to send her kid to a good school! And if the kid doesn't go to a good school, it MIGHT end up a BUM! WHAT have you got against that housemaid, HEY? Why don't you like her CHILD? What did it ever do to YOU? Think of THE kid, sir! The KID! Why not JUST. SEE. A. MOVIE?!'

Green air, green air, thought Bobby.

Then he realised he'd never *not* seen the One Man Carnival. The man was always outside the movie theatre. Day, night, dusk, dawn. Always.

How was that possible?

'. . . We've got the latest ACTION flick!' the One Man Carnival chundered. 'It's a CORKER! And talk about STAR power!'

Nobody cared, nobody listened. Only Bobby. Just this once. For Sassy.

'We've got ROMANCE! You want to snuggle, you WANT to snog? We've GOT romance movies! How about MUSICALS . . .? COME ON, you ghouls, you Blurs and night creatures. . . Can you SING . . .?'

Yeah, yeah. Bobby started to walk back to the fire-escape that led to his window.

'. . . Audition for the Firebreakers down Spillane Lane, TOMORROW . . .'

Bobby spun. A few of the not-quite-rights, the shady people, had gone. Just like that. As though they had taken from the night what they wanted.

The One Man Carnival simply kept on keeping on, as if he'd said nothing. Kept sucking in soot, insomnia and stray lolly wrappers, and spruiking all over empty green shadows.

'DON'T let those housemaids down. Think of their KIDS! We've got HORROR films, we've GOT suspense, we've GOT drama . . .!'

But it was too late. Bobby had heard. Bobby had listened.

6. A Permanent Smoky Dusk

The roof was low, the room under it wide, tumbling with the murmur of small talk. The crowd smoked, and their smoke was so thick houselights struggled to do their job. Each table seemed to blur at the edges. Each person blurred at the edges.

A band played.

They stood to the back of the main stage, half lit, like dusk, doing their thing. Giving off rambling, jazzy blue notes, taking turns at solos, breathing in nicotine, blowing out tracks. Playing like some kind of poppy, three-headed creature. Beating like one cool, half-interested heart.

One by one women made their way up under the harsh stagelights, trapped by white and red and orange. One by one they slipped into the band's groove. One by one they auditioned . . .

The crowd listened, the crowd talked. They coughed and drank. The cigarette girl kept on selling more and more smokes even though nobody needed them.

Maybe she hates everybody, Sassy thought, hiding at a table. *Maybe she's secretly trying to kill them.*

Murder by cancer. What a long, sticky wait for victory!

At one stage the soupy air ruffled. There was a shouting fight towards the back that could have been over anything. That was probably over nothing. Nobody cared. It suited the place like wrinkles on bearded fishermen.

Soon, the raised voices fell away. Nicotine and ash resettled.

The Firebreakers sat beside the stage, sometimes talking, sometimes listening, as each woman took a shot at singing over the din of a restless crowd and its foot traffic.

Some of the women were smooth, some bopped and scat all juicy and raw. Some had the slinky sway of knowledge and experience, others had pure sexuality. A few tried too hard, and some simply sang beautifully.

Each woman had her turn. Sassy was jealous. Jealous of every single one of them. But she knew, by the constant murmur of the crowd, that none had that special IT the Firebreakers were after. That luscious magic that could cool steel, romance weather, bend souls. That could sweet-talk the night and all that was in it.

That could make a hardened jazz crowd fall silent.

The night dragged.

The crowd lingered.

Bobby tried to watch them, but by now the houselights had lost their battle with the hazy atmosphere and were drowning in it. The smoke wouldn't let up. It stripped people of detail, hardened their features, buried their eye sockets, left cheeks deep and hidden.

'Mate, some of these freaks are going to give me nightmares!' he said.

'Ssh!' Sassy hissed.

'I mean it! They're all so . . . I dunno . . . Boogy, boogy, boogy!' Bobby whispered, fingers wiggling in front of him.

'*Ssh!*' Sassy spat.

'Okay, okay.' Bobby sighed. Sometimes his sister had no humour.

Scared and bored, he looked at the next table. Even sitting, the man at it was tall. Long and tall. Like old trees and large buildings.

What the hell, thought Bobby.

'Knock, knock,' he said.

The man just sat full of impossible height, lost in smoke, oozing white skin and shadows.

'*Who's there*?' Bobby persevered. 'Grew. *Grew who*? Grew-some.'

Nothing.

Bobby tried to look right at him.

'Get it? Big? Gruesome?' he said, but there was something about the tall stranger that made a person's vision slide right off him. The more Bobby tried to look him in the face, the more his eyes felt like two magnets that just wouldn't press together.

'Hey, cut it out!' he found himself saying.

It was the same with everyone there. They were solid in the corner of his eye, but when he looked straight at them, they were blurry, sitting still, watching the stage. He could hear their constant shuffle, their clinking glasses and motion, but never see it. Behind him they were talking, behind him they were moving. No matter which way he looked. Behind him. Behind him.

He could *feel* it.

They were not-at-all-right, these people. None of them.

Only the cigarette girl had unblurred edges. She looked young, yet old. Tired. As though her skin was having an affair with gravity.

'Bugger it,' said Bobby, and pinched a drink from the tall smudged man at the next table. If this place wasn't right, he wouldn't be either!

The drink tasted like nothing. Like, he didn't know . . . Like a sticky thought.

'Whoh! Jibber, jibber!' Bobby shook his head.

Suddenly, he felt wobbly, hilarious. He turned to tell his sister something funny, but Sassy wasn't there.

She was up on stage, about to audition . . .

7. White and Red and Orange

Bobby watched the crowd, who watched Sassy, who stared into the stagelights, all white and red and orange. All she could see was smoke, colour and the Firebreakers. Watching. Waiting.

Everybody waiting.

Listening.

Sassy closed her eyes, felt the thick air push against her skin. She stood there, almost safe behind the dark curtain of her eyelids, not knowing what to sing. Unable to sing. She didn't know a thing about jazz, or this shady crowd. Didn't know who they were. Didn't know *what* they were. She had no idea what they wanted to listen to.

With her eyes closed, she could feel it, just as Bobby had. They weren't quite there.

So what? Sassy didn't care. *Not a damn bit!*

All she knew, under her sweat and stagelights, surrounded by eyes and silence, was that the Firebreakers were watching. All she knew was she had this want.

This aimless, nameless want.

The band started without her. Played something boppy, universal and easy. Sassy stood there, in smoke, under white light, under red, under orange. This want, it filled her. Surrounded, smothered, drowned her! It rose into her chest. Filled it to burst.

But nothing would come out. Nothing.

Eventually, the band's song fell to silence. They watched Sassy, their eyes burning into her shoulderblades like fire pokers.

'Sing something,' Mona said. Her voice was beautiful.

Sassy cleared her throat. Her mouth opened and closed, as though she was a fish dying on deck. Open . . . Closed . . . Open . . . Closed . . .

Bubbles of noise rose from the crowd. Angry noise. Sassy clenched her fists. Squeezed her eyes shut even tighter. She opened her mouth again . . .

First, the tears came. Rich, heavy drops of liquid salt. Then this squeak. This high-pitched, embarrassing squeak.

Sassy was crying.

She tried to hold it in, but couldn't. That stupid, squeaky voice gathered. Released itself in sobs. Sobs mumbled into half-words that didn't mean anything.

And oh, oh, oh, pinned by the stagelights, that spun to red, that spun to white, that spun to orange, she *needed*, she wanted, she *want, want, wanted*! This was what her whole life was meant for. Something new, some kind of hope. She knew it! But she had no talent, she couldn't sing.

She just couldn't stop crying.

Bobby had been drinking. When he looked at the audience they seemed to be sitting upright, silent, facing the stage. But so what? Even drunk, he could hear, could feel, their raw, billowing laughter.

He pushed through the tables, the smoke, grabbed his small, sobbing sister by the hand and dragged her out of there.

8. Hallelujah

The next day was all jumbled to Sassy. She walked through it numb.
Tired. Trying not to think. She vaguely noticed the static that was
everyday talk, without taking in a single word. At school her friends
made noise about boys and acted like they were on American TV shows.

'Like, totally,' said Jose.

'Whatever,' said Maria.

The only thought that cut through any of this, that stood clear as
day, was that last night she had a chance. Her only chance.

And she'd blown it.

She hadn't even been close. Not within twenty laps of
the planet.

By nightfall, that damn ticking in her heart had returned. By
midnight it had become deafening. She sat in her bedroom, unable to
sleep, feeling its pulse in her bones, in her teeth.

Sassy felt like she was drowning.

She couldn't explain how she was feeling. Not to Bobby. Not
even to herself. She just sat in the dark, in the deafening silence,
unable to explain anything.

Finally, the last two days caught up with Sassy. She slept. Her
mind fell over a cliff, beneath dreams, into smooth, soft oblivion.

The oblivion was good. The oblivion was needed.

Gradually, drifting in the dark warm of nowhere, she felt the constant, hot mugginess of something big, insanely big, breathing all over her.

In the back of her mind she knew it was just a dream working its way down into her safety zone. She hoped it was just a dream. Half of her panicked, while the other half tried to push itself up through the thick, smothering layers of deep sleep.

In her mind — or was it her mind, was she now awake? In her mind she looked into the dark corner of her room. She could smell hot, soiled air, sticky breath. Could feel something shifting, half moving. Could hear the floor creaking under it.

Sassy wanted to scream, but nothing came out. She watched the shadowy corner, wide-eyed with terror.

Suddenly, from the street below, a passing car flooded the room with light. The shadows peeled back for a violent second. The car's high beams lit up a dragon. It was huge! Three metres tall, full of solid weight, murderous breath and bad intent.

Caught in a floodlit moment, the beast roared and lunged.

Sassy screamed . . .

Sassy sat in her bed, scattered, confused. Getting her bearings.

A dream.

It had just been a dream. Her room was dark. There was no heavy, sticky breath — just hers. Short, sharp, all confused and nervous. There was no muggy air. Just sweat. She was covered in it. The work of nightmares.

Then, from the shadowy end of her room, a voice came.

'Child,' it said, 'don't be scared.'

The voice was superb.

Mona, flowing blue velvet dress on, stepped out from the dark. Who knew how long she'd been watching, waiting? She moved towards the bed, slow and easy.

'On stage? Why did you cry like that?' she asked.

'Wh . . . Why . . .? I . . .' Sassy stammered. She was in the room with a woman who just might be a dragon.

'I . . . I couldn't find the words . . .' she said. 'Those women before me, they all sang so well . . . And I, I'm not as *good* as them. But . . . But I *wanted* so bad! I . . .'

Sassy's words trailed off. Her eyes were wide, bulging with things she couldn't explain.

'Child,' Mona said in her soft, lazy voice. 'Most of those women were just singing songs. Writing neatly on the lines when they should have been drawing pictures. Your tears had more music, more passion, in them that night . . .'

Mona stood tall over Sassy. She was intimidating, her dark brown face watching, looking down through the silence.

She brushed Sassy's cheek with the back of her hand.

'Why do you want so much, child?' she asked.

'I . . .' Sassy started. 'I . . . don't . . . It's like, I've seen something magic. Felt it. Felt this . . . just . . . magic in your jazz . . . I . . .'

Sassy knew she was making no sense, but couldn't stop. Everything everybody did around her seemed still and grey. She knew if she left that life, left the everyday, it wouldn't miss her. Not at all. It would always be there.

She had nothing to lose. She had a lot to lose. She wanted anyway.

Sassy looked down towards Mona's feet, hidden somewhere under flowing blue velvet. If only she could express herself. If only she could stop being so confused, so frightened.

'Child, you are so young . . .' Mona whispered.

'I . . . I don't care . . . I . . . I've found this hunger . . .' Sassy's words trailed off again. Tears gathered in her eyes. 'Nothing matters. I . . . nothing . . . I don't care . . . I've found my hunger,' she repeated, like hurt. 'Fear and need and . . . hunger! I've found my hunger . . .'

God, she felt stupid! The creature had wanted reasons, but Sassy was babbling.

Mona moved right in, her beautiful, black eyes blazing in the night. Sassy braced herself. For pain, injuries, for bad things.

'Hallelujah, child,' the dark woman whispered.

'Hallelujah . . . !'

Mona moved further in. She kissed Sassy. Nothing big, nothing physical. It was just a kiss. Yet, with the slightest touch, the woman's teeth drew, from Sassy's bottom lip, the smallest trickle of blood.

'There,' Mona said. 'It is done.'

Suddenly Sassy felt the weight of things irreversible. Felt a little bit glad, confused.

And very frightened.

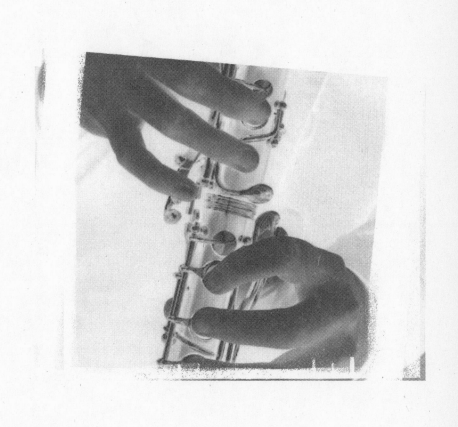

9. Mr Something

Falla Jordan couldn't play a note. But he was an okay bloke, liked good music and had a stupid name. He sat next to Bobby, puffed his cheeks, shifted and squirmed as though his seat was a skewer. He had dark, rough skin and a long, black mop of hair. Was probably Aboriginal or something, maybe Polynesian. Bobby had never bothered to ask.

Johnny Apeshit sat on Falla's other side, making a beanbag out of his chair.

Bobby looked around the room.

Two piano geeks sat up front. Lounging behind everybody were a couple of groovy boys, there to learn how to impress groovy girls. Beside them were a couple of groovy girls there to be impressed by themselves. Everybody was waiting on a little man out front.

The music teacher was new, so Bobby had decided to give him a whirl.

The teacher played his electric organ as though it was a thing of power. It swirled, churned and rose like violent midnight shore breaks.

'Gutsy,' Falla Jordan pouted.

Then the man shifted, raised his head from its buried fury, lifted the tone from flowing violence. He eased into something that bopped,

scat and jerked at the funk hidden in everyone, creating a sound
that made you want to dance like a cartoon car, putting down
the highway.

'Fairly,' Johnny Apeshit said to no one.

Soon, his music melted into a sound of silk and timelessness.

Bobby watched, listened. Said nothing.

Flowing into another style again, he finished his hello to the
class with Chopsticks.

Teacher humour.

'What's his name again?' whispered Falla.

'Mr Something,' Johnny told him.

'As if.'

'Then you remember it. Hey, ask him why he's so short.'

'Oh, okay,' Falla whispered. 'Sir?' He put up his hand.

'Yes?' Mr Somebody smiled.

'Oh, uh, sorry, nothing.' Falla chickened out.

'Everyone's permitted to speak freely in my classes,' the teacher
told the whole room. 'Music's more than just notes and chords.
There's a whole philosophy involved.'

'Philosophy? You hear that?' Johnny whispered. 'He's here one
minute and he's making a move on our groovy chicks.'

Mr Somebody let his fingers drip and gargle around the
keyboard while he talked.

'Less than half the world watches movies,' he said. 'Not every
culture has sport, or even books. Music, though, is the *one* thing that,
in some way, every person in the world has in common. The planet's
one universal language, its one glue. No matter how rich or poor,
no matter how different. Be it Russian, African, Indonesian, be it
classical, or hip hop, or —'

Bobby looked hard at the teacher. 'Food,' he mumbled under
his breath.

Falla heard him.

'Yeah. Permission to speak freely and all that, sir,' he boomed.
'But what about food?'

'Or storytelling?' Johnny added.

'Or the feel of doing a good poo,' Falla said. He and Johnny
laughed like dickheads.

'Sex is universal,' said Johnny. 'Kids jumping in puddles. Love.'

He threw that last one in for the groovy girls.

'Yeah, love!' Falla laughed.

He laughed all the time.

A lot of kids said they never cared. About the future, what people
might think of them, money, so on. But the more they said it, the more
they really did care. Falla never said it. He *never* cared. Not at all.

There was a moment of silence.

'Oh, you're *those* types of students,' Mr Somebody smiled. 'Are
you done?'

Bobby said nothing. He wanted to join in, but drew a blank.
Most of his best memories were '*What if*' dreams of comeback lines
that arrived an hour after their moment had left the station.

It bugged the hell out of him.

'I hear what you're trying to say, boys,' Mr Somebody said, 'but
I'm talking more about the arts. Things of the soul . . .'

'Permission to speak freely, sir?' said Falla.

'Always.'

'I like this permission to speak freely business, sir.'

'Shut up, Falla, you clown!' one of the groovy girls spat venom.

'As I was saying,' continued Mr Somebody. 'Music's the *one* form
of self-expression that's both art and truly physical. That requires no
pencils, or —'

Bobby stared hard.

'Sculpture,' he mumbled.

'Uh, permission and all that?' said Falla.

'God, shut up!' snapped the second groovy girl.

'He started it!' Falla wailed, pointing a good metre above the little man's head. 'Sir, what about sculpture?'

'Or surfing?' said Johnny. 'That's an art to surfers, isn't it?'

'Or sex again, sir?'

'Falla Jordan, you are *so* not invited to my party!' the first groovy girl breathed snot and ice.

'See what you've done, sir?!' Falla protested.

The teacher waited with that easy grin of his. He seemed like a nice person.

'I do hear what you're saying, but I'm trying to create a bigger picture. Music has a power.'

'*Per*mission!' Falla threw his hand in the air as if hanging on to monkey bars. 'Johnny's armpits have power.'

Mr Somebody laughed.

'Sure. But music has subtleties, intricacies, variations, emotions that . . .'

Bobby had had enough. Was starting to get angry. Music was brilliant to him, but so what? Why be a snob about it?

'Sir, can't we just play?' he protested.

'Look, what I'm trying to get across . . . What are your names?'

'Big Al,' said Falla.

'Look, what I'm trying to get across, Big Al, is that by striving to achieve your musical potential you –'

'His name's not Al, sir,' the second groovy girl said.

That was it. The teacher's grand entrance was shot. All the momentum of his music stopped, started, stopped, stopped again. Gone.

Everybody braced themselves for a spray, but the teacher was just too likeable.

'Hey, you lot,' he grinned that easy grin. 'This class *is* optional . . .'

'Yeah, thanks anyway, sir,' Falla rose, 'but I think our chips are ready.'

Johnny Apeshit lingered while his friend made for the door. He cast an eye at the groovy girls. An eye at the door. The groovy girls, the door.

Groovy girls. Who was he kidding?

'Bugger it,' he mumbled, and took off after Falla.

Bobby couldn't express himself right. He never could, so didn't try. But music felt brilliant. It was simple. That was all.

Everything.

He was sure the teacher was a nice person, a good musician. As sure as Johnny Apeshit's armpits *did* have power. But they were from different worlds.

He left without saying a word.

Bobby roamed the school corridors without a class. Lost in a place he knew too well.

It felt strange.

He never thought he might have something in common with someone like Falla Jordan.

10. A Good, Mean Wind

A good, mean wind was blowing.

It shook at trees, stop signs and baseball caps. Pick-pocketed gutters of all their garbage. Raised leaves, soot, toupées and dresses.

Bus stops leaned with its loneliness, bones chilled with its bite.

That wind, it shook at Sassy's walls, rattled the flat's windows like a prisoner shaking his bars.

Sassy loved it. Being safe in her flat, listening to days so cold and raw.

When Mona left the other night, panic and doubt had flooded in.

Sassy had raced to her window, words like *now* and *where* and *when* log-jamming in her throat.

'Relax,' a soothing trumpeter's voice had drifted up from the shadows.

'I . . . but . . .'

'You've started,' it echoed. 'Live. Take it easy.'

The voice had been so lazy. So sure. Then gone. Now, despite herself, Sassy wasn't frightened anymore.

'Sorry, honey. I hate these distance jobs,' John Piero's voice told her down the phone. 'Things are tough and there's you and Bobby. When work's there, I just gotta take it.'

He was somewhere down the coast this time. Sounded far away. Sad.

'Dad, I'm fine,' Sassy sent her voice after his.

'I stocked the fridge before I left,' he told her obvious things. 'The money's where it usually is. If you have any trouble, Wanda from next door will be stopping in to check on you.'

'Dad, you told me all this last night,' Sassy complained.

'Are you sure that —'

'Yes.'

'Wanda —'

'Will check in on us every few hours. Same as always.'

But Wanda rarely checked in.

Sassy never dobbed on her, though. Why would she? She missed her father, but whenever he was away, the place was nice and empty.

All hers and Bobby's.

'See you tomorrow, honey,' John Piero's voice told her.

Sassy turned to the window.

The wind blew hard. Pushed naked branches into a billion bony fingers, scraping and clawing at roofs and walls. Sassy took it all in. The way everything creaked and bent with its shifting, hollow weight.

She looked at the world, wondering if she could colour the wind by throwing food dye at it. *Imagine that,* she thought. *Red wind. And green and purple. The air would be filled with a hundred thousand dances.*

She looked in the closet for no reason at all. Turned over the lounge carpet, poked around the kitchen, as though each corner, each cobweb was hers to rule over.

Sassy started to feel cocky. She looked under her dad's bed.

He was a good man. He tried hard. She loved him. But maybe, she hoped, her mind racing away with the wind, he had a dark side. She knew he didn't, but why not have a look? Why not pretend?

Sassy imagined things as she rummaged through the dust. That she'd find fifty empty scotch bottles, a dead body, betting slips, guns, grenades, black body suits and trip wires. Maybe a dress he might wear when no one was looking.

Outside, the wind howled down lanes, through intersections, chewed up newspapers and fed them, page by ruffled, liberated page, to the city. It thumped at Sassy's walls and doors, as though it was determined to raze the house for clues.

But Sassy had beaten the wind to it.

She felt something hard, heavy, under the bed. Reached further, got a grip on it.

Sassy pulled out a box full of twenty, maybe thirty, old vinyl records. Every one of them wore a jazz label.

'No way!' she said to herself, as the wind clapped, banged, cheered and raged. 'Far out. It's not possible.'

One by one, Sassy worked her way through the records. They scratched, crackled and fizzed with age. Spat back little noises in the face of the gale. Most of it was old people's jazz, too clever, dull. Boring, boring, boring. But there were a couple of real, hot, sweaty tunes. She turned the best ones up. Loud! Let them fill every corner of her empty house.

Fill its thin air all fat with its own howling winds of good, tasty music.

Eventually, Sassy fell asleep on the floor in front of the record player and dreamed.

She dreamed of warm, dark places. Of smooth things. Of clarinets that blew out passionate sounds. Sounds that started in the forests, making their way to the cities, to her city, by which time they had blown themselves into howling winds. Winds that pushed against closed windows, against blocks of flats and container ships, that made everybody walk with a tilt. That leaned on the world.

Winds that, if you could just untangle them, would moan the most beautiful, most lost of songs.

When Sassy woke, night was settling in, all rough and uneasy. She opened the window, invited the wind in. Danced with the dark air and billowing curtains.

Bobby was at the turntable, playing some of the loose records that Sassy hadn't checked out yet.

'How were your drum lessons?' she asked about his latest musical effort.

'I'm giving up,' he said. 'A rattling exhaust pipe has more rhythm than this teacher!'

'Giving up? Already?' Sassy protested.

'Just on the lessons. I can't be stuffed with them.'

'Why did you choose drums, anyway?'

Bobby remembered that day with the Reptile. Drums had a power about them. They never apologised. The idea of them was simple.

'I dunno,' he said. 'They're gutsy.'

Bobby played more music. More jazz and mystery. Sassy danced.

'You know, some of this stuff ain't half bad,' he said, as his sister swirled. 'For jazz.'

'Har, har,' Sassy mumbled, still full of sleep and dreams. 'This wind is great.'

'Yeah,' Bobby agreed. 'We should be out in it.'

'Sure,' Sassy told him. 'We'll hit the roof.'

She headed for the window as a new song started. Then stopped dead.

'What? What is it, Sass?' Bobby worried.

Sassy turned her head.

'That record you're playing . . .?' she asked. 'Who is it?'

'Dunno. The label's blank.' He shrugged, the wind pushing his hair up and crazy, as though it was shocked without him. 'Who cares?'

Sassy's eyes went wide.

'Listen!' she gasped. 'That voice . . . It's Mona's!'

11. Music and Silence

Sassy's room was dark. Its silence hugged her in good ways.

Bobby was snoring, of course. So was her father, back from
work again. But they always snored. They were hopeless. Two
hacksaws buzzing away at the night. Sassy had lived with it all her
life. It didn't sound like anything anymore. It was the neighbours she
felt sorry for.

John and Bobby could buzz all they liked. The world was still
quiet.

Sassy made her way to the dark of the fire-escape, to watch
the white streetlights, the red tail-lights, the splashes of neon. She
wondered where the Firebreakers were. What to do about them?
Declare war or give in to their music?

She wanted . . .! She want, want, wanted!

Wanted jazz, midnight romance! But they had done something to
her. Mona had done something to her.

Her heart raced at night. Sometimes her bones seemed to shift.
Grew heavy or long or strong. She would feel movement, bending and
twisting, within her blood and skin. Bolt upright in bed only to find
her limbs still the same. Her arms still arms.

Weeks had passed since Sassy discovered Mona on that record,
but no way was she going to ask her father about it, about Mona. Not
until she'd figured out how much trouble she was in.

Was her mind playing tricks, or had Mona's kiss somehow infected her blood in strange and powerful ways?

It rushed and pumped through her veins. She would go all flush for no reason, want to tear up the boys at school. Then, suddenly, she would feel ordinary. The same as always. Like Sassy.

Only music soothed her. Music and silence.

Eventually, Sassy stopped thinking and let her mind wander out her window, take a walk without her.

The air felt good out there. Still and timeless.

She had always woken with the music alarm, had the radio on in the shower, the Walkman in her ear on the school bus. At school there was school talk, friends or TV when she got home, CDs to fall asleep to. Everyone she knew was the same.

She'd never realised it before, but her and her friends must have hated silence. Been at war with it.

Now here she was, not plugged into electricity. Without her friends. In the silence.

Feeling strong around it.

It felt like a place to move and breathe, carried some kind of power. Each night, more and more, the silence felt like a stage for music. An empty canvas.

'I'm ready,' she whispered into it.

And, for once, the silence heard. And sent something from the dark to fetch her.

12. Stairwells and Moods

Sassy was in an unlit lane, facing the back end of a laundromat. Driers hummed, gave off heat the cold winter's night needed. Plumbing hugged old brick walls.

A crummy little apartment sat on top of all those washers and driers.

A skinny man with a ginger goatee and hammock eyes stood in the doorway above the old wooden stairs.

'Hey, kid,' he gave a lazy smile.

Sassy could see white walls in the room behind him, jazz posters. Some were the right way up, others upside down. Some were facing the wall. She had no idea why.

'You're that trumpeter,' she said.

'Raglus,' he smiled more.

'Are . . . are you really a dragon?' she asked.

Lost in shadows, the trumpeter hesitated for a second.

'I'm a half-breed,' he said. 'The skin's a giveaway.' He rubbed at his flesh-tone scales and scratched his rusty beard.

'But . . . Mona's skin is so smooth,' Sassy said.

'Mona's a pureblood.'

'A . . . I don't . . .'

'Purebloods aren't diluted. Not half anything. They can still change.'

Sassy had no idea what to say. She knew there was something more to the world, but when someone talked like the trumpeter did, it sounded so stupid.

Absurd.

Sassy heard the wash of traffic, the hum of driers, smelt the rot and damp of an overheated lane. One of the other Firebreakers walked up past her. The skinny one. He had a clarinet in his hand, a good-looking face, rough skin, spiky peroxide hair.

'Here's that punk mix you asked for,' he said, slotting a tape into Raglus's pocket as he passed. 'Hey, you made it!' he smiled a goofy smile at Sassy before disappearing through the door.

Sassy's brain finally grabbed at something it could understand.

'Punk?' she protested.

'Sure,' Raglus said. 'Some punk, old punk, has real power. Real honesty. Honesty's important. You can hear it.'

Sassy was in a whirl.

She was scared, unsure, and now this trumpeter was talking about a form of music that hated trumpets with vicious spite.

Sassy hung onto the old wooden railing, cat piss and mould in the air.

Behind her, somebody's dog, trapped in a shoe-box backyard, snarled and barked through a crack in a fence. Down where lanes met, a stereo pumped *Doof, Doof, Doof* from a bedroom. In the distance, an ambulance siren clawed at walls. Two TVs competed for sound. Somebody's toilet flushed. Neighbours argued over who farted.

Bobby would have loved it.

'How do you escape all their noise?' she asked.

'How do they escape mine?' the musician grinned.

'But . . .'

'Besides, I like it. The thin walls. There's something more . . . human . . . about them.'

Sassy thought about that one.

Gradually, she could hear the rich sound of a woman singing. Could make out some kind of tone, an almost light, not quite sea green, not quite murky blue, coming from one of Raglus's two rooms. It reminded her of dreams you can't remember, of the bits of life without words. Of a memory that had no moment or event.

'Have you ever wanted to travel in a mood?' Raglus asked in the dark.

Those sharp teeth of his showed.

'I . . . I'm not sure . . . what . . .' Sassy said.

The singing voice seeped into the lane and all its noise. The trumpeter held out a casual hand.

'Lesson One,' he beckoned.

Sassy's feet trembled as she walked up the stairs.

13. White Light

Bobby's room was white with sunlight when he woke. That meant he was late again. He waded through his garbage, scratched, slapped out a noiseless tune on his lap.

Late was late. Why fight it?

Eventually, colour came to his room. What a mess. He rapped out a beat on Sassy's wall, but heard nothing. Figured she'd left without him.

Rare, he thought.

Bobby walked through the white morning to his grey school. He heard three songs on the way: a pop tune from the radio of a delivery truck, the tinny sound of a metal song from a passing Walkman and an old Greek man whistling a Madonna track.

Good stuff.

Inside, there was no white sun, no music. School was still school.

'Where's your girlfriend?' the lady at reception pushed her words out.

'My sister's already here,' Bobby told her.

'Why are you late?' she said, as more kids lined up behind him.

Routine, routine, thought Bobby.

He hated it. Why did she bother with these late slips? Neither of them cared. Whatever reason he gave, neither of them would believe it.

One day I won't bother to give an excuse, Bobby thought. *I'll simply dance and jig, like a puppet on a string. Just stand here dancing and jigging until the Principal comes out and smacks me in the back of the head.*

Today, though, Bobby had started his day with a cool song or two and white light. Best not kill his good start.

'You see, my cat —' he started, even though he didn't have one.

'Here.' the receptionist gave him his late slip. 'Next.'

Routine, routine.

Lunchtime dodged and weaved, did a good job of hiding from time. Eventually, though, the school bell found it.

Bobby hit the yard to look for his sister. To talk the talk, chew the fat. To say 'Hi' and move on. He checked her crow's circle of friends, the milk bar, the park.

But she wasn't anywhere.

14. Hugs and Sorrow

'Dad!' Sassy burst through the door.

She leapt at him and hugged him, hair all over her smiling face.

John Piero hugged his daughter back, all happy and confused, a dopey smile on his round head. It felt great to be embraced like a father.

'I missed you,' she sighed into his chest.

'Gee, well, I . . .' he stuttered, as he rubbed his hands through her hair. 'I . . . didn't see you at breakfast. That must have been some day you've had!'

'Oh, Dad. You're beautiful!' Sassy sighed again.

'Where have you been this afternoon?' he said. 'Bobby's out looking . . .'

John Piero's hand slowed to a stop. Something wasn't right. Sassy's hair was too long. She seemed taller. Stronger. The way she told him he was beautiful like that, as though she knew things, as though she was wise, or he wasn't . . .

Hell, he knew he wasn't. But . . .

He pulled back and looked. She smiled at him, glad, but now also sad. He had left for work yesterday, in the early morning, not seen her since he'd kissed her sleeping head goodbye. Now she was older.

Much older.

Then Mona strolled through the open door.

'*You!*' John Piero pointed a rage-filled finger. 'What have you done to my daughter?'

Mona just looked at him through smooth, half-open eyelids.

Sassy's dad fumed. He bubbled and seethed and knew a passionate man would not stop to think. He knew a passionate man would tear Mona down if he could and figure things out later. The *who*s, the *what*s, the *why*s.

But even then, even with his daughter aged without reason, experienced in motion, in tone, literally overnight, he tried to think what reaction would be the right one. That would hurt Sassy the least.

'How . . . how much time have I lost with you?' he pleaded to his daughter who was still hugging him desperately.

'I . . . I don't know . . .' she said. 'Time was strange. A year . . .? Maybe only six months.'

'Only . . .?' John Piero held up her chin.

'Dad,' she pleaded. 'I'm not old. I'm still a girl.'

'Only . . .' he repeated, full of sadness, as if that was enough.

John Peiro took his daughter by the hand into the lounge, pushing past Mona, his shoulder knocking her back.

He sat on the couch, holding Sassy's head in his chest, and cried.

'When I heard them, Dad, that night, in the lane,' she said, 'they were so good, so smooth. I . . . I don't know. Jazz can be old and boring . . . but, but not this stuff. When I heard this stuff it was like I'd always loved jazz. Always.'

John Piero kept his head low. Said nothing. Stroked her hair. Whispered, 'Sshh . . .'

He went into his room, reached under his bed. Pulled out his old jazz records. Held the one born in mystery. With no label on it. With Mona's voice trapped in it.

'I played these to you when you were a baby,' he said. 'When you cried. When it was time to sleep. When you woke. To ease you into the day . . . '

'Why . . .?' Sassy asked.

Somehow, Sassy had aged. Had a steel about her. A strength her father never did. He was lost, sad, didn't know what to do.

So he simply told her.

'Honey, when I was young, I met someone, or . . . or they found me. This someone was just . . . was so . . . I can't . . . She sang and we became lovers, and she left. She came through, drifting into my life, then out again, like, I don't know . . . like weather. I couldn't find her. But I had secretly stolen her voice . . . Trapped it.'

He held up the record.

'To . . . to have had something, something so . . . so . . . I couldn't figure out what this . . . beautiful . . . smoky woman, saw in . . . By the time I stopped asking why . . . she wasn't . . . Then you and Bobby came along. And all I had of her was this vinyl I'd made without her knowing.

'You hated thunderstorms when you were a baby. They made you cry and cry and cry. So I would . . . would play you this . . . stolen jazz, and sit and rock you . . .

'You were my excuse, baby. My excuse to remember.

'I gave you a taste for it when you were young, Sassy. I'm sorry . . . It's all my fault . . . Six months to a year . . .? More . . .? Suddenly, I've missed you. I've missed you so much.'

'Oh, Dad,' Sassy hugged him harder. 'Why did you stop playing that music . . .?'

'It was too much for me, honey. I *had* to give up hope. It was wrong. I had you and Bobby . . . And I *did* love your mother . . . I'm so slow! . . . I didn't realise how much wrong I was doing her, filling you and Bobby with my yearnings for dragons. Not until your mother had passed away . . .'

'Dragons?' Mona said from the doorway.

'I knew. How couldn't I?' he replied, in a hard voice, not taking his eyes off his daughter's long hair. 'A blind man could see it. The way you move, breathe. The way you stand . . . I knew,' he repeated, with bitterness.

'To be honest, I don't remember you,' Mona raised a lazy eyebrow.

John Piero looked at her, bursting with fierce, short-round-plumber rage.

'Lies,' he growled.

There wasn't much to say after that. Mona left. John Piero sat on the end of his bed with an old photo of his wife and said sorry to it and regretted. Sassy climbed up to the roof to breathe, to sing with that breath. Sing soft, sing scatty, create city music with city air. To let her voice roam, soothe her, while she tried to think things through.

It didn't much help, but she kept singing, without knowing why. Kept singing just because.

Gradually, she noticed it was raining.

15. Talent

The weather was outside, doing its thing. Good on it. But everybody was in the school canteen, going off, tapping feet, dancing, cut from the real world. All curtains drawn.

They cheered and grooved while three young dudes played their guts out, hogging the tiny makeshift stage.

'What do you think?' Mr Somebody yelled to Bobby.

He had the hugest grin. It was almost eating itself.

'Well?' he waited.

What did he want Bobby to say? *That they had talent?* Sure. The room was pounding with it. They had talent by the truckload. *That they had looks? That they wore good, lazy threads?* Yeah, they seemed cruisy, like they had no tags on themselves. *That they had that sound?* The *in* one? *Full of energy, yet smooth? All alternative radio?*

Big deal.

Mr Somebody raised his eyebrows. He wanted an answer.

'I dunno. Whaddo you think, sis?' Bobby avoided him by calling to his other side.

Sassy was at school today, but not. She seemed bored, was thinking of other things, jazz things, dodgy things, didn't even hear her brother's question.

Bobby watched the band more. Listened more.

They seemed tight. Even when they cut loose, on the slide guitar, on the bass, on the drums, they were tidy. They smiled and loved it and were in love with it and going places.

Everybody loved them because they were smooth and tight and going places.

Students and teachers stomped and clapped and hollered. The groovy girls preened themselves in front of the bass player because he had dreadies.

Good luck to them, Bobby thought, and meant it. *Good! Luck! To! Them!* Somebody had to make it.

But . . .

The band started another song, pushed right past the end-of-lunch bell. Everybody cheered. Even the school's biggest thugs accepted they weren't the centre of attention for a while.

Only Falla Jordan broke ranks. He stood in the doorway, laughing, yelling 'Less! Less!' every time a song ended.

'Well?' the teacher refused to let it go.

'I hate them,' Johnny Apeshit said from behind them both.

'*Why?!*' Mr Somebody protested.

'Why?' Johnny yelled back. 'They're too smooth, sir.'

'So?'

'So I'm not, sir!'

Bobby looked at Johnny Apeshit. At his bad teeth and lazy clothes.

Damn, he thought. *That was a good answer.*

16. Dreams and Hunger

Sassy was falling. It was a dream. She knew it was a dream.

But couldn't stop falling.

There was a light-blue sky: pleasant, everywhere. A thunderous rush of motion, a wind-tunnel, made by her, plummeting through the still midday nothing.

At first she was frightened. Terrified. She knew it was a dream and tried to wake.

But kept on falling.

She felt her lips move in her sleep. 'Jesus. Oh, sweet Jesus!' But she couldn't wake.

And Jesus wasn't flesh and blood anymore. He was gone. And all that was left of the old world was weather and earth. And all that was left of the dinosaurs were sharks. And all she could see of magic was jazz and things that lived in cracks and shadows.

Sassy was falling.

Horrified. And got more serious than Jesus.

'Dad,' she whispered. 'My new blood, I'm scared. Help me.'

But Dad wasn't there, because she had been young and brave and, oh, so stupid. And had made a decision. Cast a tiny, powerful want into the dark and found the dark a real thing.

And she was dreaming.

And falling.

Falling through the light-blue sky of black dreams, and whispered with all her might: ' Mona . . .'

And then Sassy remembered she was hungry . . .

She turned, lost her fear and fell into the approaching water, blind with that hunger.

And there was a shark. A White Pointer. There was blood. Blood everywhere! Teeth and flesh and ripping.

And, somehow, when the blood cleared, she was still there, in the water. Still all there.

And no longer hungry.

Sassy was awake.

She stared at her ceiling in a cold sweat and screamed as if to shake loose all the glue in the world.

She screamed with fear. She screamed because her dream felt good. Because it tasted good. She screamed until her voice ran right out of petrol. Until all the air in the room was sick of dealing with her.

And somewhere between her waking and screaming herself dry, her father had appeared.

And was comforting her.

17. Drum Kit

Bobby was the only person in the classroom.

He sat right in its goddamn middle, slapping and thumping away at his school books with drumsticks, all fast, easy and hopeless.

He bashed and seethed, let some kind of mood buzz around him.

Eventually, the Principal walked by. Did a double take in the doorway. Bobby glanced at him and kept on slapping.

'Where's your class?' the Principal finally asked.

Bobby kept looking at the blackboard, looking at nothing. Kept drumming. He thought about things for a moment. His sister was drifting away, spending less time with him. Not answering his easy questions. Not talking. Not with him, or anyone from school. He'd still knock on her wall in the mornings, but more and more often she wouldn't be there.

Suddenly he realised he was furious.

'Come on. Where's your class?' the Principal demanded.

'I don't know, sir,' Bobby told him.

The Principal's job was to be Authority, to make snap decisions and brass them out, no matter how stupid. That's what they'd taught him. Most of the time, though, he was bluffing.

There was something about the way the boy played. He was bad, but didn't stop, like most people who are bad at things do.

The Principal liked it. The way the boy had forever.

'So, should you be in a class now?' he tried again.

Bobby stopped playing. Looked at him.

'I don't know, sir.'

The Principal thought about it, scanned the corridors one more time. Nobody had seen him. Safe was safe.

He left Bobby to it.

Bobby slapped and smacked at his books. Harder and harder. Thought of nothing. Was glad that man had stopped hovering in the doorway, like the Emperor with his thumb facing sideways.

All Bobby knew was that the Principal was the enemy.

All he knew, surrounded by the slap of drumsticks, was that, for the first time in his life, he was angry.

18. Videos and Pinball

John Piero winced as he walked into the video parlour. Every game in it was full of popcorn and fist fights, daring anyone or anything to step near them. Each one as loud as a carnival, as violent as a landmine.

He looked around. Nothing moved, despite all the noise.

The room wore a permanent dusk. Clocks were useless once you stepped into the video parlour's blurred tones. Playing money was the only way to measure time.

The plumber found his daughter laughing, cheering, having a ball in the seat of a racing-car game. The man in the seat beside her looked serious. He had olive skin, wore loose clothes, was plucking at a mandolin, a double-bass case at his side. He seemed like one of those people who had seen tragedy, yet remained friendly and strong.

'Honey?' John Piero said.

'Dad!' Sassy leapt into a hug. 'What are you doing here?'

John Piero looked at his daughter. She was still small, still thirteen. But wasn't. Something in her was gaining speed.

'Me? Doing here? I don't know.' He scratched his head. 'I kept hearing things. Voices, or . . . I couldn't . . . In the background. Keep seeing . . . in the corner of my . . . Almost . . .'

'I don't . . . They told you to come?'

'I . . . dreams . . . half fell asleep on my lunch break . . . Thought I almost . . . heard . . .'

The man beside Sassy stood up. Took the conversation away from the fumbling father and fumbling girl.

'I'm Palestine, sir,' he gave off a calm, serious tone. 'We sent for you. Your daughter would like to spend some more time with us.'

The video parlour crackled and popped like computerised eggs and bacon.

'. . . Excuse me?' John Piero growled.

Sassy leaned into him. Held him.

'Please, Dad,' she said. 'Please. I need to . . . I just . . .'

'Honey . . .'

John Piero felt someone watching him. He turned expecting to see shadows, like he had a lot lately. But there was a thin young man a few games back. Handsome, with high cheekbones and spiky blond hair.

'That's CT Virus, Dad,' Sassy tried to smile. 'He plays in normal bands, with uni students and stuff, as well as the Firebreakers! He's real friendly, and . . .'

But CT Virus didn't look friendly. He watched with no expression.

John Piero scanned the room, its dimmed light and flat, throbbing screens. Some kind of not-quite colour seemed to swirl and rise, like steam. Behind Palestine a solid Asian woman with small blank eyes turned from playing pinball.

'Oh. That's Jodi, Dad! She plays drums, just like Bobby!' Sassy rambled. 'She only likes pinball, though! They all do! None of them will play the video games!' Sassy laughed. 'Isn't that crazy?'

'Sassy . . .'

'I mean —'

'*Sassy*,' John Piero looked at the jazz musicians. They all looked at him. He knew what they were. They knew he knew. Sassy knew. Yet, only his daughter didn't understand the gravity of it all.

'I can't just —' he started.

'Oh, please, Dad!' Sassy dropped all small talk.

'Sassy —'

'*Please!*' Sassy wailed.

She put every shameless, grovelling drop of emotion she had into that small word, shifted it from a request into a hopeless, desperate cry for help. Gave it so much heart John Piero could feel its blood and veins.

'*Please!*'

John Piero felt the musicians watching. They didn't matter. His daughter did. She was everything, his whole nine yards. This want of hers was so big it gave her pain.

'Sassy . . .'

'I . . . I've *got* to go with them! Just sometimes, Dad . . . A week here or there . . . Miss a bit of school . . .'

'Now, wait a —' John Piero pointed.

'Dad!' Sassy gripped at him, Sassy bounced. 'They want to teach me about jazz. About *music* . . .! Didn't you once love music . . .? Not just the playing . . . All of it . . . Imagine, Dad . . .! I . . . All of it . . . *Imagine* . . .'

Videos gargled and burped their sirens' song to all the coins in the world. Nothing moved in the heavy light. Eyes watched, eyes burned.

John Piero scratched his bald plumber's head, fretted and worried. He couldn't think straight.

'Trust us,' Palestine said.

John Piero didn't trust any of them, not as far as he could vomit uphill. He watched the Asian woman, who watched him. There was something about the way she stared.

John Piero looked at his daughter. Her hunger wasn't magic, it was real. Ageless.

But Sassy was just thirteen. But she wasn't. He didn't know what to do. It drove him mad!

Jodi stared.

John Piero looked into his daughter's eyes.

'I trust *you*,' he said.

'Promise?'

The moment waited, like a drop that wouldn't fall.

'. . . Yes,' he pouted in defeat. 'For now.'

Sassy hugged him, short, sharp, full of love.

'We should be going, then,' she said.

'I . . . Hey . . .! I . . .' John Piero stammered.

'So, everything's sweet? Good stuff,' CT Virus grinned. He placed the gentlest of hands on John Piero's shoulder as he passed. Now he looked like the friendly, easygoing person Sassy said he was. 'Thanks,' he beamed.

John Piero was lost. His mind felt like it had been released into cold water and was gasping for air.

He had taken the longest three or four minutes of his life, forever, to agree to things and had been dropped, in a second, like old news.

Suddenly, he worried. He worried, he worried, he worried.

But it was too late. A promise had been made.

19. Chinatown

It was late. Neverending late.

The moon hung itself over the city, looking through the spaces between buildings like squares stand on tippy toes to watch a party over their fence.

Bobby was in Chinatown, where time was trapped by tired streetlights. They flooded the footpath in a permanent electric dusk, everything humming with a colour lost somewhere between tired orange and pale yellow. Every shop looked as though it was built around a small tank full of sad crayfish in a red neon window.

It had taken Bobby a lot of walking, a lot of listening, on bored, solo nights to get this far. To realise dragons might be found in Chinatown.

Bobby walked, looked, listened for jazz, for his sister. For anything.

People dressed fantastically at night in Chinatown, fit, like romance, into the dull electric light, yet the lanes were full of bad smells, unlit, bursting with the clatter of restaurant kitchens that sucked in air through flywire doors. Kitchens full of leather faces, sweat and half-dollar wages.

Chinatown reminded Bobby of an impossibly handsome person with rotting teeth.

All beautiful and ugly.

The lane he now stood in was no different to the rest. It made noise, it steamed, it sweat. At its back, behind a fly-wire door, a kitchen crew worked in a panic. The garbage bags stank.

When Jodi walked out from the steam to sit on a milk crate and have a break, Bobby was there to greet her.

At first he just watched.

Chinese women, to Bobby, could be the most beautiful in the world. Yet the Firebreakers' drummer was ugly, bloated with size. She had the smallest eyes, sitting there, buried, in the biggest of frames.

Her off-white chef's outfit, its pencil-stub hat, made her fit in with the sink and black garbage bags.

'Why do you work like this?' Bobby asked. 'The Chinese love dragons, don't they? You could be a God?'

Jodi looked up. Recognised him from that night of sweet summer rain. She stared at him as though he was small. Or the question was.

'It not work that way,' she said. 'Us, the orang-utan, the tiger. There be reasons we become rare. Best we stay hidden.'

'But —' Bobby started.

Jodi pulled a pair of drumsticks from her chef's apron, held them up at him. She slid one around the rim of an empty lard drum.

It made a simple, grinding sound. Fluent, yet not remotely smooth.

Then she slapped the other down. Killed the first one's roll. Killed it sweet. Then she rolled it again. It felt like she was making a musical sound out of wet cement.

She killed it with a slap.

She rolled it again. Faster. Killed it. Faster. Killed it with a double beat. Wound herself up.

Then, with one last grinding roll, her wrists and sticks fell into music, while she stayed solid, sitting on a milk crate in the smelly dark.

Suddenly, everything was machine guns.

Jodi rained and tickled on that lard drum. On the sink, its pipe, the milk crate. Sounded like a 50-garbage-bin wind-chime caught in a storm.

Then she stopped with a two beat. With shotgun breaks.

Then released a roll and grind. Wet cement, wet cement. Tickle and tease. Build and grind and fall and blur and rain.

Heavy rain. Smooth rain.

Slapping, smacking, falling rain.

And there was nothing, *nothing*, smelly or dirty about that small, dark patch of lane. Everything was a sound. Every wall an echo, a backbeat.

It wasn't loud. None of it. You had to be close enough to see it. To feel it. Jodi never thrashed. Her arms barely moved.

Then she wound it down. The slaps eased to a trickle, a spit, a drizzle, slowly slipped off all solid things.

Stopped.

There was the clatter and bash of a busy kitchen. Clipped Chinese voices. General noise and silence.

Jodi tucked her sticks away. She looked good, ugly, strong.

'I get three-minute smoke break,' she said. 'Don't smoke.'

'But —' Bobby started.

'Later, little thing,' Jodi told him. 'After work.'

20. Know Your Magic

Bobby walked with Jodi through the electric yellow-orange mood of Chinatown. Along the side streets, down the lanes. Surrounded by the continuous wave of kitchen noise. Hissing woks, clattering plates, barked food orders. Brilliant sounds.

Bobby had never noticed them before, but now he was aware of them, they were everywhere.

All Jodi had said to him when she finally downed her mop, put out the last of the garbage and knocked off for the night, was: 'Home.'

And he had followed.

'Home' sounded cool. Caves, monsters! Rock on!

They walked.

Bobby said nothing. He was amazed at how many questions he didn't have about the Firebreakers, or even dragons. Suddenly, for some reason, he didn't want to know how old they were. Didn't want to know *what* they were.

He didn't want to know what they ate, what they could do, how they looked so human, what the whole jazz thing was about.

He just didn't care.

The Firebreakers had nothing to do with today. There obviously weren't many of them. The ones that were about were more of an echo, too tough to fade or bend to tides, living strong, breeding.

Evolving, adapting, to flesh and music and the human world.

They were a proud cluster, a proud breed. Those few that were left.

Hang on. Clusters? Proud breeds? Why did I think that? Bobby thought. *How did I know that? I don't know anything. It's my specialty.*

Bobby couldn't figure out why he didn't ask where his sister was. She'd been gone for a week. Was she in danger?

What was this incredible pressure he felt these days, like someone was always watching?

Like bad things were on the way?

They walked.

Bobby wasn't a details person. He hated details. They were against his religion. But, for the sake of his sister, he needed lots of them.

Yet every time he went to ask, he kept yearning for the click of balls at his local pool hall, feeling as though he shouldn't care.

He looked sideways at Jodi as they walked. She had a strength about her. A strength bigger, older, than her chunky frame. All the Firebreakers did. As though they were pillars of rusty steel and muscle.

Bobby could picture his sister, still the same, still little, surrounded by two or three solid beasts. And three or four half-breeds, descendants, who looked mostly human. In his mind they stood around her, facing outward, guarding. It wasn't easy, guarding. But they were trying. Would continue to try, fight and give their lives, like the Earth refuses to give up on gravity.

It was the best they could promise. But a promise. And promises were gold.

Hey! Bobby thought. *Earth? Gravity? Promises? What the hell?*

He looked at Jodi again. She walked with the same blank

expression, the one that said there wasn't much behind those small, black eyes of hers.

Every time Bobby lined up questions, his ears imploded, his brain rotted and entirely different answers seemed to melt into his scull.

'Are you messing with my mind?' Bobby asked her.

She walked. Said nothing.

But Bobby could feel someone, some*thing*, in his head. Throwing up ideas not his own.

They walked.

Bobby saw his sister as a small lion, or a big cat, out there somewhere. In a huge, thick jungle of sorts. And he was stumbling after her, without a clue about jungles. Blind, mute, stupid. Fumbling about, in jungle traffic, surrounded by jungle dangers, with nothing more than half-tuned city ears to guide him.

God, who's watching out for who? he thought, looking up at Jodi again.

She seemed all dumb and bloated. But Bobby was learning better.

Maybe he should get the hell out of there.

Now, why did I think that? thought Bobby.

'Stop it!' he yelled, wiping his head free of non-existent cobwebs. 'This is screwed!'

Jodi turned and regarded him. Looked down, a lock or two of jet black hair hung loose around her wide face.

She was huge.

The Chinese Dragon stared and stared.

'Here,' she said, then scribbled something on a takeaway napkin, hardly used. 'Help your sister? Know *your* magic.'

Bobby looked up. Their walking had taken them into the lane

opposite his place. *How was that possible?* His place was miles from Chinatown. They hadn't walked a quarter of the way.

He looked back. The lane crossed three short blocks, then turned at right angles, like it always did. Yet from that right angle came the orange-yellow hue of Chinatown, a city away. And there, in front of him, was his home, everything painted sloppy green neon.

He could even hear the One Man Carnival.

'COME ONE, COME ALL! LEAVE THE NIGHT ALONE, SIR . . . !' he yelled at a group of boys. 'YES, YOU LOT! YOU'LL JUST END UP BROKE AND DISAPPOINTED! SEE A MOVIE! COME IN FROM THE WORLD . . . !'

'Well, well, well,' an acid voice suddenly hissed.

It was the busker, the one with the pork-pie hat. The Reptile. Standing behind them, in shadow.

'I'm not interrupting anything, am I? You know: kissy, kissy, kissy . . .?' he pecked his impossibly thin lips.

Jodi said nothing. Seemed to steel herself, rather than face him.

'Three little drummers in a lane . . .' he crooned, scraping at his snare drum. 'How cosy . . .'

Bobby's throat went dry.

Mona, the Firebreakers, they were problems. But this, he knew, was trouble. Big trouble.

21. Punk

Bobby bolted up his fire-escape, eyes wide. Scampered through the green neon of his bedroom window.

Suddenly, everything was still. Silent, save his V8 heartbeat.

'Unreal!' he breathed.

He would have said more.

'Sassy, your friend and the busker stared at each other. Just stood and stared. Stared, like, I dunno what, like . . . I dunno. They just stared.'

He knew his sister.

'No way,' she would have goggled her eyes.

'And, and, there seemed to be a man and a woman and maybe someone, or something, or something else, in the shadows behind the busker,' he would have goggled his eyes back. 'And, and, a block away, a policeman turned his head and walked towards the lot of them.'

'I don't believe you!' Sassy would have said.

And Bobby would have known it all sounded like garbage, like fantasy and bullshit, but he had seen it with his own eyes, so would have insisted. And she would have believed him. *Believed* him! Just like that.

If only for family, for loyalty.

'And, and, the policeman seemed to stand not too far behind

Jodi. And the, the loud man from the cinema, whatever his name is, stopped spruiking and watched,' Bobby would have stammered and gushed. 'Everything was, like, y'know . . . Just . . . y'know . . . still.'

Bobby would have used sound effects to tell his sister about the sudden, mad thrust of movement, quicker than reflex, before anybody was ready. About the one-second clash. Seeing the Reptile on the ground, hurting.

He would have used his eyes to get across the feeling of brewing shadows.

'And, and when the policeman drew his gun . . .' he would have said.

'*Drew his gun?*' Sassy would have squawked.

He knew she would have squawked.

'Yeah,' Bobby would have told her. 'I bolted.'

'And?'

'I bolted!' he would have insisted.

And he would have told her about that last glance he took. About seeing the busker crawling away, on elbows, back into shadows.

He would have felt like a hero as he told her. A legend! Just for seeing it.

Eventually, when he'd calmed down, he would have even told her about the raw-as-guts punk song that kicked through his head as he watched it all. About how everything, in that moment, was thumping, relentless symbols and drums.

He would have told her about the weirdest bit, the colour between the Chinatown lane and home. The colour that wasn't. Wasn't sea-green, wasn't murky blue. Just wasn't.

Bobby knew Sassy would have wanted details. Not just of the weird stuff, but of Bobby's punk song. She knew he loved gutsy music. She knew him.

He knew it.

He would have repeated the song to her, even though he didn't know the words. Acted its energy, sung its noise. Used his chest for guitar sounds, arms for drums, head for vocals. She was his sister, he could explain things to her that way.

'Hey, don't you have *anything* to do with the Firebreakers!' he would have told her. 'They're *way* too dodgy.'

But he didn't tell her. How could he? She was away again.

22. Goth Girl

Sassy's friends had given her a new title. The Wag Queen.

She had no idea how much school she'd missed. Years? A few days? Time had become strange to her. If she could carbon date gossip she'd put it at a week, no more.

Whatever, the crows' circle — she, Jose, Julie and Maria — settled on the concrete steps overlooking the yard. Like always. Took in their lunch break. Talked like they knew the world.

But all Sassy knew was school made her feel sticky and grey.

'Hey, look. There goes Goth Girl,' said Jose.

'Who?' Julie scanned the yard.

'Louise Alfonse.'

They all turned, looked at a small skinny girl in long crimson velvet as she walked, unsure, across the neverending concrete schoolyard.

Louise Alfonse had once been plain enough. Invited to the Everybody things, the bigger, *who cares* parties, nothing more. Now she looked all new, nervous. Her pale face and black lipstick lost in an everyday schoolyard.

'Check her out! She just looks stupid,' Julie moaned.

'I hate Goths. I hate Goth music,' Jose agreed.

'What sort of music do they listen to, anyway?' Maria asked.

'Who knows?'

Boys ran around. They smoked, threw balls at each other, kicked balls away. Missed and scored goals, hoops, service breaks.

'It's moody,' Sassy said. 'Dark and, like, theatrical. Full of black images and sorrow.'

The girls all popped their eyes.

'What the?' Jose wailed.

'I don't like it,' Sassy said. 'I just know a bit about music.'

'Well, aren't *we* the expert.'

'I didn't mean it that way,' Sassy said, looking at her shoes.

'So it's bad?' Maria asked.

'It's sort of serious-daggy,' Sassy said. 'I dunno. It's just not me.'

'Who cares?' Jose protested. 'This is Louise! I bet she's not even into that music. Look at her! Now everybody thinks she's a freak. Why would you do that to yourself?'

Sassy watched Louise nervously cross the yard towards her new Goth friends, who were all smiling, posing, comparing Goth jewellery, Goth things, walking in ways only Goths know. Being something different.

Being something the same.

'Maybe she wants somewhere to belong,' Sassy said to no one.

Maria watched with her.

'Yeah. I don't know,' she said. 'Maybe.'

'Ftt!' Jose killed the topic. Jose loved killing topics. Her ambition was to be a door bitch one day. 'Have you seen that student teacher? Yum! I know where he lives! I'm going to climb through his window!'

'As if!' laughed Maria.

'Sure. And what?' agreed Julie, and the crows' circle was away again.

Sassy joined in as best she could, but her ears had kicked loose from her brain. Were flapping in the wind, pointing at no one. She heard her friends talk about how gross Johnny Apeshit had become, but they sounded distant, faded. She heard a Rapper on somebody's radio, the squawk and chatter of schoolyards.

She heard nothing at all. Not really.

Just kept looking at the Goths, and from there, everyone.

Sassy looked, Sassy looked.

The Goths weren't the only music cluster in the yard. The Mainstreams hung with the Mainstreams, Rappers with Rappers, Hippy Fossils with Hippy Fossils. The Metal Heads with Metal Heads.

Alternatives with Alternatives.

They were the worst. So high and mighty, so obvious. Good luck to them. Their music was great, but so what? They used it to divide themselves into types, just like everybody else. Nobody broke ranks. Not really.

Nobody.

Sassy looked.

She felt claustrophobic, couldn't breathe.

She cut from her friends. Crossed the playground alone. She grabbed Johnny Apeshit with her newfound strength and pinned him hard, holding him in close in a way that made it look like neither of them were resisting.

Even though he had no say in it.

Sassy closed her eyes and pashed Johnny Apeshit. Let the world fall to black and kissed with the Garage Slob to wash her Mainstream friends out of her hair. To fight against sameness. To stop her soul from flaying about. To breathe.

To save herself from drowning.

Somewhere in the dark of closed eyes, Sassy felt her new blood pounding like thunderstorms. *It boomed, it boomed!* It scared her. Between its maddening beat, she heard her friends snigger, gasp and protest. Could feel everybody watching. Alternatives, Geeks, Metal Heads. Everybody.

But she kept her eyes closed, kept herself out there. Breaking ranks.

She kept kissing Johnny Apeshit, as if to hide all the raging energy and confusion of her world.

23. Dead Leaves and Lolly Wrappers

School was over, everybody had gone home. Hung themselves in the sun of milk bar doorways, spread themselves across video parlours and parklands, planted themselves in front of their TVs and stereos.

Bobby found Sassy behind the school, where the yard-duty people never came. She was propped against the grey cinderblock wall, sitting in dead leaves and lolly wrappers.

'Hi, Bobby,' she mumbled from behind tears and long drooping hair.

'Who is this stranger talking to me?' Bobby replied.

'Sorry,' Sassy moped.

'You could have told me you were at school today.'

'I said sorry.'

'No worries,' Bobby said, trying hard to mean it.

There was a moment's silence. Nothing but a cool breeze. Time. Dead leaves. The grey of the wall.

Bobby thought he saw something sitting on top of it, above his sister. When he looked it was empty. Just a wall.

'. . . I pashed your friend. Johnny,' Sassy told the ground.

'I heard.' Bobby smiled.

'I . . . I can't hack it.'

'Hey, Sass. Waddo I care? If you like him, then —'

'I don't like him! I don't know him. I can't hack . . . I . . . These kids, and their talk and . . . and everything.'

Bobby said nothing. He could have sworn there was someone just behind and to the side of him, beckoning to his sister. But, no, there was nothing there.

'I just want more . . .' Sassy said. 'Don't . . . don't you ever . . . I mean . . . Want to be lost . . . And . . . Want more . . .? Don't you ever want more?'

Bobby was sure there was someone to the other side of him. He turned.

Nothing. No one.

'You're starting to sound like a fancy pants, Sass,' he said. 'I mean, school's something to do. To fight against. It ain't so bad.'

'Bobby, it's . . .! I just . . . *Bobby!* Help . . .! I don't . . . I . . .' Sassy cried, Sassy cried. 'I'm not just a kid anymore, Bobby.'

'Yes you are.'

'I . . . No . . .'

'Then what are you, sis?'

'. . . I . . .'

'What are you that makes you so special?'

'I'm not special! I'm not! I just . . . Music . . . I can't tell . . .'

'C'mon, Sass,' Bobby gave. 'What are you then?'

'I . . . *I don't know* . . .!'

Bobby watched his sister. Head down, she stared at her outstretched hands as though they were dead, strange things. For a second he could hear what she did. Felt this monstrous pulse in her veins.

He stepped back, heart racing.

Then the moment passed, like stupid thoughts and fantasy.

'Look, everything's okay, Bobby,' Sassy brushed off her mood. 'I gotta go. Practise, practise, practise, y'know.'

'Sure, sister.'

'*Gotta git, gotta git, gotta git git git right outta here . . .*' Sassy sang.

'You're crazy,' Bobby touched her drying tears and messy hair.

'I know,' she smiled.

Then Sassy left. Walked down the lane, away from lolly wrappers, dead leaves and grey cinderblock walls.

Bobby looked right at her back as she went. Looked hard. He thought he saw shadows dart for bins and rusty garage doors, away from his sister, into the far, far corners of his eyes.

He didn't know why, but it made him smile.

The crisp, nothing-day breeze picked up. 'Prick,' he thought he heard a voice carry through the distant, grey air. But when he listened hard for it, there was just the distant sound of peak hour.

24. Swampy Guitars

Nobody had fixed the orange neon sign for a week. It blinked on and off in the pet-shop window, giving the hamsters stress and relief, stress and relief.

Bobby watched them.

Orange and dark, orange and dark. Scurry and breathe, scurry and breathe. Orange and dark, orange and dark. Scurry and breathe.

'Bugger that,' he grumbled.

Bobby thumped the window so hard it cracked. Became a spiderweb, just like that. The neon light didn't just stop, it popped. Shattered.

One hamster died of a heart attack. One went into shock. The others scurried and swirled harder and faster than ever before.

Bobby watched them.

'Jeez . . . Sorry . . . I didn't mean . . .'

Then the last, dangling bit of neon fell and the shop alarm went off.

The blue light in its corner thumped and thumped, the siren beneath it wailed and wailed.

'I . . . Jeez . . . What . . . Little fellas . . .'

Bugger it. Bobby bolted.

'Sorry, little fellas!' he mumbled as he ran.

When Bobby finally found the band venue, it was just a band venue. A pub. It had muddy cream walls dotted in sticky tape where bands had put up posters and the owners had torn them down and the bands had put up more and the owners had torn them down and so on. Each weekend a high tide of hope rose on them. Each morning a low tide of business fell.

The security man was just security. There was nothing *boogy, boogy, boogy* about him.

Bobby could hear the muffled sounds of a band, could feel the venue's heat and smoke as he stood at the door.

'ID,' said the security.

Bobby fished out Jodi's napkin. It had the band venue's name scratched into it, all sloppy, as though written in the dark. Nothing more. He handed it to the man with the warm back and cold front as though it was a gold key.

The security screwed it up. Bounced it off Bobby's head, with a cute little slam dunk. Chewed his gum and thought of other things.

'ID,' he said.

'But I —' Bobby started.

The security raised his hand, as if saying *wait a minute . . .* forever.

'No I —' Bobby tried.

The security held his hand out again. A little more to the left.

'I really —'

And again. To the right. He was enjoying himself.

Bobby looked around and through the security. The man was used to that. All those lemmings sticking their necks out, wobbling their heads up and down to either side of him. Doing the *How Can I Get In* dance.

'Could you just —'

The hand went up and to the left.

'No, I have —'

Low to the right.

Each time Bobby tried to spin a line, the man deflected him like bullets.

'Sneak in the back windows?'

'Locked,' the hand went up, the gum was chewed.

'I'm a friend of —' Bobby started.

'Everybody is.'

'What?'

'A friend of.'

'Who?'

'Whoever you were going to say you were a friend of. Everybody is,' the security said, looking past Bobby. 'Give it up.'

Bobby rocked with hopeless anger. The security was used to that, too. The *Anger Wobble* almost always came after the *How Can I Get In* dance. Now he was waiting, bored, for the *Epileptic Rant*. The one where Bobby would try the one about having big brothers that would rip the security's head off. Or maybe he'd try the *Slinky Loo*, the one where he would ask if he could just go to the toilet and he'd swear he would be right back out again.

Both of them waited for Bobby's next crack at it.

The gum was chewed. The hand was ready. But Bobby changed tack.

'Were you a kid once?' he asked.

'Sure.'

'How would *you* have got past you?'

That was a good one, the security thought. He'd pay gold to hear something new. He looked at Bobby. Really regarded him.

'This is my job, kid,' he chewed his gum. 'Here come tonight's main band. Work them over a bit.'

'How?'

'Tell them you're a really big fan and ask if you can pretend to be their roadie. They'll love it.'

'You reckon?'

'Sure. Tell them they're *gutsy*!' the security smirked.

'Are they?'

'Who knows? I don't really listen anymore. But most bands love being told they're *gutsy*!'

Bobby tried.

The band did love it. They looked like five leather jackets with stubbly humans poking out of them. They laughed and scratched and let Bobby carry their equipment into the place.

'He's with us,' they insisted to the security.

'Thanks,' Bobby said to him.

'No worries,' he chewed his gum.

He didn't really give a damn one way or the other. Now Bobby was the band's fault and problem.

Bobby stood behind the greasy video machines. There was no doubt about it, the place was just a band venue. Nothing more. Inside, the posters stayed up, because they were cheaper than wallpaper or a new paint job.

People tried hard and said things.

'No rent, dude.'

'Look at me, I'm so drunk.'

'The coolest, man!'

'Then he said, then she said, then he said.'

'I hung out with their guitarist, man!'

'Their last CD.'

'*No*, drongo! Pot the three ball, *then* the six!'

'Don't tell me how to play pool!'

Yadda, yadda.

It was all music-scene talk. There were no secret codes in what they said. There were no blurry people, no trap doors to places Other. The barman was no monster. Nobody had the presence of dragons.

Know your magic, Jodi had told him.

Bobby couldn't see any. Not anywhere.

He looked more.

The crowd was half a crowd. A mix of regulars, of rockers and technos without a nightclub, a sprinkling of Goths. Bobby loved Goths. Their white skin, their layers. He wouldn't be one, wasn't friends with one, but he loved them anyway.

He relaxed a bit and moved towards the stage, in with the crowd. Opened his ears to the music.

The support band was loud, ripping out some kind of psychobilly sound. A growling old world mix of rockabilly, punk and grunge, held together by fuzztone and feedback, pure garage, scraped off the belly of slimy fat men.

Most people seemed to be there because it was a place to kill a night. The lead singer didn't care. He thrashed and wailed to his true believers of dirty music. He grumbled and howled, had a great voice, great moves. Hunger to burn.

But just couldn't get his microphone right.

He would grip it so tight it came loose, knock its On to Off, strangle it with his rage, bang it into his head, drop it time and again, thrash and growl so wild it rarely caught his voice. He was intense. Hopeless.

The more Bobby watched, the more he loved it. Loved it like gravy!

The man let rip his songs from the body, from the soul. Mikes were just made for mouths. Bobby doubted there was one in the world that could do him justice. That could capture him, or his volume that came from head to toe. The stage vibrated. Everything was guitars, anger and thumping drums, as though the band was bashing, no breaks, down a pothole-filled highway. Heads and pool balls shook as the song peaked. Instruments spat, volume cut and stung. The man screamed like the damned.

He crashed around his mike, knocked its lead out, fumbled with it time and again until, finally, he threw it to the floor, threw his arms wide and yelled the final few punching lines.

He yelled free of body. Not trapped or contained by microphones, or what other people would do, or anything. He yelled as though his rage could carry his voice over his band's thunder. As though there were more important things than shelter or money. As if anger, rhythm and craziness are all the food you need.

It almost worked. He almost pulled it off.

But the crowd couldn't quite hear him over guitars, drums and amplifiers.

Bobby didn't care. He loved it! Loved that moment! It was sensational! Everything to do with everything. CDs would never capture it. Never! Squares would never know. The sound quality was poor, the worst, half the song's words had been lost. But so what? Noise rained, noise rained.

This was energy. Pure, angry energy! Raw, dirty power.

This was Religion. Hopelessness!

And Bobby was sold.

Feedback faded down leads, back into speakers. The song finished. People clapped, people got drinks, went to the toilet, chatted each other up. There were no ghouls, no shadows that talked.

There was a band venue.

A band.

Music.

This was Bobby's magic.

The next song oozed out from amps, onto the stage. Built up like mudslides, then poured onto the floor. Started with swampy guitars, swampy guitars. The lead singer gurgled and growled.

Bobby loved his music, its energy. The gutsy simplicity of it all.

25. Purple

Somewhere across town, Jodi looked into a shadowed crowd. Into the Blurs, the Others, the humans. She played drums and gave them her small black, blank eyes.

Her sticks tapped away at a cymbal, trickled and spat all over an inch of its frame. They ran soft and sweet, telling the murmuring, hazy crowd they were jazz-bound.

Soon, Raglus joined her, brought his lazy hammock heart to the stage. His trumpet folded and peeled itself into a neverending solo, curling around ears, slipping under doors, into storerooms and toilets and lanes.

He played, and cats and drunks for miles rolled on their backs and started to purr.

Sassy and CT Virus waited in the purple shoebox of a band room, for Raglus's neverending moment to end.

CT came from Hungary. So he said.

He lay back, staring into the purple ceiling and did for Sassy what the others wouldn't. Not even Mona. Smouldering with dark thoughts, he gave up some of his mystery.

Told Sassy a tale.

'When I was a kid . . .'

'You were a kid?' Sassy said.

'Sure.'

'When?'

'The twenties,' he said, like nothing at all.

CT Virus waited. Breathed.

He would inhale, smooth, and smoke would exhale, smoother. Drift, like memories, from the edges of his mouth, into the nothing.

Even though he wasn't smoking.

Sassy watched him. His high cheekbones, his baggy pants, his tatty peroxide hair. Only his voice, deep and rich, gave away his insides.

Raglus played, Raglus played.

'When I was a kid, I hated all the stuff on the radio without knowing it,' CT said. 'But I listened. Loved the songs I only liked, just to have something to love. Just because everyone else was loving songs and I didn't want to miss out. You know?'

Sassy did.

CT Virus's breath continued to ooze up, in thin lines, to molest the ceiling.

'My father wore his human skin well. He was a blacksmith. He liked the heat, liked the flames.'

'But I still don't . . . School . . . I mean . . . you know . . . your skin . . .' Sassy tried to keep up.

'It was Europe in the twenties. A village. Not everybody went to school. After the war, some kids had skin worse than me. I worked for my old man.'

The clarinet player waited for more questions.

When there were none, he waited for the rhythm of his memories, for their four-beat, to come around again. He watched his breath. Watched the past.

Watched nothing.

'My dad had this radio. Back then they were big, like a bar fridge,' he breathed. 'But, living in the hills, the best we could get was this spot on the dial stuck between two distant stations. He'd listen to two muffled songs drifting in and out, and static, all at the same time. Every day. He was one of those types, it just didn't bother him.'

Up on stage, Raglus curled his trumpet around Jodi's backbeat, that carried it ducking and weaving through small talk, where it could spread itself wide. Conversations wound down. People swayed.

'Dad just liked having noise there. Company,' CT continued. 'It drove me mad. Eventually, even though I never liked the music, I guess the way the songs mixed made me listen. All those same old tunes became something unpredictable. It was good to know music was going on out there. A world of it. It was good to know I might really love one of those songs. If only because I couldn't really hear it.'

'I don't know what you mean,' Sassy said, all honest.

CT Virus smiled.

'Have you ever fallen in love with a boy you only saw at a glance behind the wheel of a passing car? Wondered about him for weeks?'

'Oh . . .' Sassy said. Of course she had. All the time.

CT smiled.

'Then they killed my father.'

'Who did?' Sassy protested.

'It doesn't matter. It was Hungary between wars.'

'It *does* matter!'

CT Virus gave Sassy hard rage and sorrow eyes. Somehow, just looking at them made her know she was being rude. Fanning raging fires.

'Sorry,' she said.

The clarinet player watched the ceiling until his eyes were lost again. He waited, in the square, purple band room, for the length of a four-beat, and another.

And another.

Soon, smoke dripped and trickled up from his nose, became solid, grey breath, as he refound the rhythm of his story. He ran his mind to its speed and slid back into its journey again.

'I'm a half-breed. A descendant. I wasn't born with many pure-blood senses, or loyalties,' he said. 'I hid my skin as best I could, took over my father's furnace. Gave up on youth and listened to that damn radio, stuck between static and songs.

'The Shades, the Blurs, the scratchy, distant sounds, they knew what I was. They courted me and stalked me, but so what? They do that to most lonely people and children. Then, one day, one night, in weather and rain, I heard a song on the radio.

'One song.'

Raglus bound air into a single note. Raglus pushed it through brass, into collarbones and minds.

'This song was some kind of rockin', boppin', scattin' jazz tune. Washboards and swing, playing through raindrops, attacked by static, almost smothered by the other station's song. But it was there, in the night. Something different. Something I liked not just because there was nothing else to like.

'Oh, man, that music, *that song*! It was some kind of door, a door to something more. Something to learn. Be lost in. To explore.

'Freedom,' CT Virus stood up as Raglus's solo wound its way down. 'One song. One door.'

He looked at Sassy as if he knew she was thinking of that one night. That rooftop. Of hot nights and cool dragons and sweet, sweaty summer rain.

She watched him back. Watched his perfect, skinny face and rough, scaly skin. Watched him breathe smoke and barely contain his naked firestorm of rage.

'It felt so good,' he said, 'to discover my dragon side.'

Sassy looked at CT Virus, standing there. She looked at this blacksmith's son, this dragon's boy, and somehow knew he was living his life as fun, as forever, as possible, to get back at those who killed his father.

The half-breed just stood there, breathing. And his breath, the passion of his tale, bubbled, peeled and warped every inch of purple paint in the room.

His long thin fingers worked their way around his clarinet. Stretched and tweaked into its hold spots, its grooves.

'Between work, I learnt, I learnt. I played and played in my father's shed, into all weather, into snow and heat. Into Hungarian storms that started in Turkey and blew through to the Siberian plains. Storms that crossed oceans and times. I played and played until, one day, Jodi stepped out of the rain . . .'

The purple paint crackled and popped behind him. Melted and curled.

Out on stage, the crowd had been hushed. Raglus's trumpet faded into Jodi's cymbals, which faded to nothing.

The slightest murmur, not a sound more.

Now, it was CT Virus's turn to greet stagelights and polite applause. Then, in a song or two, for a song, no more, it would be Sassy's.

The clarinet player's face relaxed into that sexy, goofy smile that fit, easy and fun, under earrings and spiky, blond hair. He looked at the little girl in front of him before he left.

'Do you know how old Mona and Palestine are, Sassy? You and I are so unbelievably young! We have forever. *Forever!*' he said, smoke everywhere, paint oozing down the walls. 'How lucky are we to be saved.'

Then he made his way up on stage. And played.

And had a ball.

26. The Poster Cave

Falla Jordan had put an ad on the noticeboard about auditioning for a band. That was three days ago. Now Bobby was nervous. He'd been practising hard. He wanted this.

Bobby looked around Falla's room. The walls were covered with posters stolen from light posts and pub windows. The place was lead-heavy with them. They made Bobby feel like he was in a cave. The cupboard, the ceiling, even the bedroom mirror had a poster over it. The Monaros, whoever they were. Falla had cut out the lead singer's face and written next to it, *You are here!*

Bobby tried to see his reflection in the mirror where the head had been, but it was too small. All he could see was his left nostril.

Falla and Johnny Apeshit walked in from the lounge.

Johnny Apeshit had looked the goods when he first came to school. Safe and boring. Enough to make little girls moan. But each day he hung with Falla he seemed to fray more and more.

The pair of them were laughing about something. Falla laughed all the time. It was a good laugh. Never too long. Just loud and generous, then gone.

'Okay. We have a few tests for you,' he said, then laughed.

Bobby made his way towards a drum kit Falla had probably rescued from a wrecking yard.

'Nah, not those sort of tests,' Falla laughed.

'Here,' Johnny Apeshit said, then thumped a tape into the deck. He cranked it so loud the neighbours became part of the song by banging on the wall. Its volume shook the roof. Posters fell. Guitars and pouting lips and hard-arsed sneers came tumbling down.

Falla scratched at his dark skin. Laughed. 'Do you like it?' he yelled.

'I can't . . .?' Bobby touched his ear.

'LIKE!? IT!?' Falla heaved out one word at a time.

'YEAH! GUTSY!'

Then Johnny Apeshit turned it down. Way down. To a trickle.

'Is it still a gutsy song?' he asked.

Bobby had no idea what they were on about.

'Who cares?' he guessed, like a joke. 'Now it's not loud.'

Falla laughed through his hair, like some people breathe. He and Johnny took fake notes. Nodded and made mock points to each other, like they were big business.

Falla laughed again. In a short, sharp, dead-pan burst.

'One more test,' he said, as Johnny left the room.

Soon, Johnny re-entered the poster cave with a bowl of water in his hand. Placed it in front of Bobby.

Bobby looked at it. They looked at it. Falla laughed.

'Play something,' said Johnny.

Bobby looked at it some more.

Play? On the water? The ripples would . . . You'd have to have so much control, such touch . . . These blokes must be so good that . . . I'm nowhere near . . . he thought.

He had no idea how to tackle this. None at all.

The clock was ticking.

Bugger it, Bobby said to himself. He grabbed his drumsticks, and, under poses and perms and Hendrix and tattooed arms and rock'n'roll emblems, under posters and posters, he rained down hard on that bowl!

Water kicked up, made a sneering band cry. It splashed on a few CDs, wet Bobby, Falla and the floor.

Falla and Johnny stood there laughing.

'You're in!' Falla cried.

'Ta-dah!' Johnny threw his hands in the air.

'But, don't you want me to show . . .?' Bobby looked at the drums. 'I mean, see if I can . . .?'

'Nah,' Falla laughed. 'I mean, who cares? I can't sing . . .'

'And have you heard my guitar . . .?' Johnny agreed.

'Sorry about the tests. We were just dicking you around,' Falla confessed, then remembered he hadn't finished his sentence with a laugh. So laughed.

'Ta-dah!' Johnny threw his hands in the air again.

They both fussed over the tape deck.

'I can't believe someone answered our ad,' Johnny said, as he strapped on his guitar.

Falla laughed.

'So, who's going to play bass?' Johnny asked as he cranked up the PA.

'Oh. Bass. You reckon we need one?' Falla said, all serious.

Johnny tweaked a string. His guitar looked like an old tennis racket that could make a bit of noise.

'Need a bass? Dunno? Who cares? We've got a band!' he cheered and started playing something none of them knew. Not even Johnny. It sounded like he was strangling a cat.

The ceiling shook, another poster came down. The one on the window. Light tried to get through, saw the room and thought better of it. The neighbours started thumping on the wall again.

Falla pointed in their direction.

'We wouldn't need you,' he said to Bobby, 'if they would only do that when we played on the road!'

Then he laughed.

And sang.

And was terrible.

Far out! I'm in a band . . . thought Bobby, as neighbours thumped and posters peeled and Johnny Apeshit played God-knows-what and Falla wailed as if in his own world.

He saddled up behind the drum kit. Sat on a couple of old milk crates and got into it. Thumped out anything.

Good and hard.

27. Silence and Spoils

Spring blundered into the city, all dumb and unaware of itself. It tripped people up with its mood swings. Rained on lunch breaks and shone on peak hour. Had no clue about personal space or body language. Sassy lay in the dark, on her bed, staring at the ceiling.

A cool song unwound from her tape deck, like a midnight octopus, through patches of quiet air. It wasn't jazz or country or rock. It wasn't anything, it was everything.

It was emotion.

Bobby lay on the floor, staring at the same spot as his sister. Both of them looking through the paint and plaster, to worlds beyond.

'. . . and then he farted!' Sassy laughed. 'That Palestine! He's so serious. But he farts *all* the time . . .'

'How long are you home for?' Bobby asked.

'Tonight,' Sassy told him.

Bobby said nothing. He listened for the One Man Carnival the way a street might check for its heartbeat. The man was there, but distant, as though still spruiking while on his coffee break somewhere. Footpath traffic talked. Not-quite-rights argued over not-at-all-right deals. They were just static. All noise was, except the tape-deck music, slinking around the edges of sound.

Somehow, Sassy's room kept a nice silence at its core.

'This band's called The Spoils,' she said.

Bobby didn't care what their name was. He'd never heard of them and knew he never would again. They were too real for radio. But for this one night it seemed they owned the world.

'Have you seen Dad?' he asked.

'He's sleeping.'

'He left some money out for you.'

'That would be handy.'

Bobby took in the silence some more. Kept his eyes on the ceiling.

'I can't believe how quick you're learning to sing,' he said.

'Quick?' Sassy protested. 'It's taken years . . .!'

Then they both realised what she'd let slip.

She looked at him sideways. He sat upright. Stared hard at her. She was maybe a fraction taller than last time she was home. Nothing more.

'Tell me,' he finally asked. 'Just how old are you now?'

'I dunno,' Sassy said. 'It doesn't really work like that. Only parts of time shift. A lot of me is still thirteen or fourteen, or whatever.'

Or whatever, thought Bobby.

'Unreal.'

Sassy's song twisted and turned. Did its quiet thing.

'How's school?' she asked.

'The same,' Bobby sighed. 'Two plus two still equals four. Some sums are getting harder and have more numbers, more squiggly bits. But, basically, the left side equals the right. You know.'

'Uh-hu.'

'Tell me about the places they take you,' Bobby said.

'Places?'

'When you're gone. You're never here anymore. Tell me about *their* world? The towers, the gargoyles, the caves?'

'*Listen . . .!*' Sassy bolted upright. 'That's her!'

Bobby listened. Somehow, the fantastic song on the tape deck had faded, deferring to other noises out there, in the night.

Mona was singing.

Singing soft. Singing superb.

And the not-quite-rights and the bums and the security-car CDs and the hum of electricity, all the back-noises of a metropolis seemed to be sucked down the throat of her backbeat. They all gave her silence. True silence. The wind dropped dead, air became thick and still.

The night had healed.

All that was left was a distant, beautiful voice drifting through the empty streets and lanes.

'Listen to her, Bobby,' Sassy said.

Bobby went to the window and could hear Mona, feel her magic, her jazz, but couldn't put his finger on something.

'Wow,' Sassy insisted, her smile growing in the dark.

Her song? What is it about her song? Bobby thought. Mona's voice, it carried the perfect timing of centuries, the flow of moonlit waves. But . . . *What?*

'She's so . . .' Sassy smiled more. 'Primal.'

Then it hit Bobby like a right hook to a pug boxer's dumb head. Nothing but smooth, rich sounds flowed from Mona's mouth. Just like on that first night, she wasn't singing any words.

She *never* sang any words.

'I haven't been anywhere, Bobby,' Sassy said.

Then it hit Bobby like another right cross, followed by a thousand left jabs to the groin. He looked out the window at a small silhouette of a tall dark woman, on a roof, some two blocks away.

Watched her sing, watched her sway.

These dragons with their jazz, baying at the night, their caves were their apartments. Their taverns were our pubs, used in the in-between seconds of time. Cities were their mountains and ravines, streetlights were their moon-filled mists. Skyscrapers with all their grey logic and money and rules were the castles of Camelot.

Their nemesis. Their enemy.

Dragon slayers.

There *were* strange places beyond they travelled to, but, for the most part, those places beyond were found in the cracks of this place, this world, this time.

Their never-never was right here. Right now.

Their blood was their home.

Suddenly, watching Mona sing, Bobby thought she looked more like a wolf, howling at the moon. And everything about her – her voice, manner, presence – was huge.

Just huge.

'You'd think . . .' he said, coming back down to earth. 'You'd think they'd be angry. Y'know? Angry at being trapped in this practical world. That they'd like rock'n'roll.'

Mona sang, Mona sang.

Sassy sat on the end of her bed, in love with it all.

'Jazz can be angry,' she grinned like a child. 'It just doesn't need electricity.'

Mona sang. Sang through heavy, still air.

Then a hard, cold rain came down.

28. The Faraway Chatter

Sassy hadn't been home for over a week. It was becoming too hard.
She stood on a roof, in the dark, scat and bopped to herself,
chewing on her music like cud. Distant voices whispered around
her. They mixed themselves into and under the sound of a rattling
aerial and distant TVs, while down across the street squares
bashed and thumped on Falla's wall. The faraway chatter
annoyed her, but every time Sassy turned, the rattling aerials
were just rattling aerials. The TVs were just TVs. There
was no one there.

She watched her brother through a gap in the window of the
poster cave.

She listened . . .

Johnny Apeshit moaned.

He was trying to shape Falla's fingers over the strings of a guitar
that looked more like roadkill.

Finally, he planted each finger just right. Told them to stay.

'Wow,' Falla laughed, then wiggled them all over the guitar's
neck like a drunken spider.

'No, no!' Johnny Apeshit lunged at him. 'Don't pretend you can
play! Just hold them there and strum!'

He hunched over, pushing, bending, trying to bend Falla's fingers back into place. They resisted like rigor-mortis, did their own thing. Played at being dumb.

Falla looked down on Johnny.

'You already have a guitar. Shouldn't we have brought a bass?'

'This was only five bucks,' Johnny Apeshit said.

'I can see why,' Falla laughed.

He turned, stuck his arse out and farted at Bobby.

Bobby, trapped behind the drums, threw one of his drumsticks at the approaching fog. It bounced off Falla's head and back to Bobby who, surprised, caught it with a chest mark.

'How cool was that?' Falla said, rubbing a spot above his eye.

Bobby tried to push the air away from him as though there were worse fates than dying. He gave a four count and the band let rip.

Then everything was serious and brilliant.

Falla thrashed at his one chord, sang without a microphone. Johnny Apeshit butchered sound, Bobby pounded. Their music bounced off posters, ceilings and walls, thumped back into itself, shook its head with surprise and kept going. The two guitarists stood either side of Bobby, facing each other, staring at nothing. Looking into space beyond being poor loud boys.

Everything was volume. Everything was noise.

Neighbours bashed and cursed. One made his way to the front door to argue with Falla's dad, who looked big and angry and argued right back, both of them shouting over solid, sloppy music, arms waving, eyebrows raised.

Falla, Johnny and Bobby didn't notice or care.

They hammered it! Pushed and pushed and pushed without going anywhere.

They're the worst! Sassy smiled.

The song thundered and rolled until it seemed to give up, as though the room's volume had been wrung dry. The three of them stood there, looking at each other as the last of the feedback faded into the walls.

Just stood, grinning, in cocky silence.

Falla laughed.

Sassy stood in the dark. Watched over her older brother. Visited him with her eyes. Scat, scat, scat to herself the whole while.

She was jealous of them. Of Bobby and his friends. Their music seemed so simple. Hers was tied up with so much other stuff.

Bobby and his mates cranked it. Belted out another tuneless tune. Laughed and yelled.

Sassy thought about her father. About Mona. She decided that passion wasn't for good or bad. It simply didn't care. It was too strong to care, had no idea of consequence.

But it drove you.

Passion consumed you with amazing, desperate energy. Gave you victories. Gave hunger that gave power to those victories. It gave you moments to be lost in. Mona *was* passion, a smouldering, rich flame. But she burnt things.

Sassy thought about her dad.

Love cared.

It gave you moments to be remembered, built on, savoured. It compromised. If it was true, it gave you pride.

Sassy had never realised how love and passion could be in such conflict. It was heartbreaking.

The band played.

The neighbours argued and phoned police and had no need to be so stuffy and every right to be angry and hated being angry and enjoyed being angry.

Bobby seemed to just do. And love it. And not care.

29. Boo!

The Blur was well-faded. It moved through streets, between shadows. It strolled.

It kept its eyes and ears open. Slid through lanes. Hovered in empty doorways. Smelt for jazz. Grovelled for music. It prowled behind and around the vision of the solid world.

People walked by. The corners of their eyes kept slinging it forward. Again and again. Shortcuts to nowhere.

Then, within its whir, it heard a

Rat-a-tat-tat . . . *Rat-a-tat-tat* . . .

It heard a steely

Hisss . . .

A tinny little rhythm, an intro beat, that it followed through the cracks in people's sight to a dumpster, in a cramped, empty loading bay.

Someone was there.

The Blur shuffled into the corner of the drummer's eye. Looked at the person from side on, saw his faded yellow suit, the snare drum, the dead-eyed stare. Then its world swirled and churned. Volume and sight became a rapid smudge of black and grey.

There was another person there, in the shade of a roller door. They were staring ahead, without expression. Carried no music at all.

The Blur was cramped for shadows, for places to exist, between the two strange men. The music tugged at it like a moth to flame.

The snare made noise.

Rat-tat-a-tonk-tat-tat . . . Rat-tat-a-tonk-tat-tat . . .

It picked up its hard pace. Added slide and groove. Sounded like a hollow, funky thing. All cold and urgent.

The faded yellow man moved centimetres to his left. The Blur, as was its way, shifted in kind. It pressed itself well into the swirling edges of the drummer's view. Where it could breathe, where it was safe. Where it wouldn't burn.

Then a third person opened their eyes. Another cold face.

The Blur felt a deafening impact.

Hurt.

Screaming hurt.

Greys whistled and bent and moaned. Silence shivered, rats bled. Echoes howled.

The Blur was trapped. Pinned in a triangle of hard, unblinking eyes. Surrounded by plain sight. There was no doubt for it to slide into, no angles in which it could breathe.

It felt cold hands reach for its arms. It thrashed.

'Why?' it said.

But its voice became a distant thing. The squeak of a clothesline.

Then, with a small click, a flash of white light ripped and tore through its heart.

It screamed!

It screamed and screamed and screamed! Screamed into the silence, into the void. Into mysteries and music.

It screamed to jazz and dragons and things like itself. To music that might soothe it, to creatures that didn't mind it wasn't really there. And being a Blur, its scream got lost under screeching car tyres, mingled with the hiss of cat fights, was drowned out by the flush of toilets and the beep of bus doors opening. Became an almost sound, that if you listened too hard for, wasn't.

People shuddered in their sleep, felt it thrash in their dreams and nobody quite, really, heard it die.

The man in the faded yellow suit knew he was sending a shudder through all things Other in the city. Knew he was feeding small nightmares to good and bad dreams. His mouth stretched into a nasty, frost-breathing grin.

'Boo . . .' he whispered.

30. Red Lights

The man's name was Wilson.

He was tall, yet solid, had an ugly, friendly face. Wore blood-red stagelights and two-dollar clothes.

When he sang, the world stopped, consumed by envy. Vines grew. Love slid down. People unsure about their musical talent gave up in comparison, or burned with his immediate, head-on challenge, clutched at like straw, seized like gold.

When he sang, people changed, people grew, people fell.

Sassy watched the cracks and shadows of his red soaked face, his forehead, hidden eyes, mouth all pushed into deep song.

She felt a sense of loss and lostfulness. Of fragility and inspiration.

Wilson sang, and his voice soothed, his voice boiled. People who needed to believe in things were embraced by it. Found a home.

When he sang, his voice spread out and surrounded and drowned. It filled Sassy with yearning and peace and power.

Once or twice, between songs, Wilson talked.

He rambled on, all easy, about visiting circuses and elephants being kept in abandoned schoolyards. About tough neighbourhoods and friendly queues. Lining up with smiling, talking thugs, homeboys and old Italian ladies to collect elephant poo for your yard. He made the everyday seem brilliant.

Then he sang again.

Eventually, Wilson's set ended.

Some of the small crowd left as if nothing was any big deal.
Others pushed through the tables and chairs to talk to and worship
him. Some drank. Wilson seemed like a man with no money in his
life or ways. No attitude. Just honesty and dry humour. He talked and
drank with and quickly became one of the crowd.

'Well, what do you think?' Raglus asked.

'He's great,' Sassy said.

Her voice sounded all wrong. Like her words were only words.

'Do you want to meet him?' Raglus asked.

'You know him?'

'Sure.'

'Is he, like, a half-breed, or something?'

'No. I met him when he was driving cabs. Wilson's just a friend.
He helps me out now and then.'

'But he's not jazz,' Sassy said.

'Sass, I'm older than jazz,' Raglus grinned. When he spoke like
that, Sassy could feel it. His age. His impossible lack of age. 'For me
it's not about this type of music or that. A song either is or isn't gutsy.
You know?'

Sassy didn't know. She loved *jazz*. Loved it! Not blues, or rap, or
whatever, or garage.

She felt frustrated without knowing why.

Wilson's voice was the deepest, smoothest, most solid thing.
It preached everything she believed in — fragility, strength and
pride — but what would she say to him? *Gee, you're grouse?* No.
There were enough people pounding that into him already. Besides, it
wasn't awe she felt, it wasn't worship.

What then? Sassy thought.

The afterglow of Wilson's voice burned into Sassy. Her insides churned. She searched them for the right words and could only find one.

Jealousy.

Wilson's voice had made her insanely jealous. Jealous of him and it and the types of music that inspired it. That didn't even grab her. She was jealous of his passion, his world.

'No. Thanks, but not yet,' she replied.

Sassy left the small venue and found a spot on a warehouse roof. Where there was just her and Raglus and blurred shadows, hovering and whispering around the corners of her perceptions. Where there was silence. Where she could practise, practise and practise.

A place where she could rise to the challenge of rare, beautiful sounds.

31. Scrubbing and Disco

It was Saturday.

There was a band Bobby wanted to see. A party he wanted to go to. When he'd asked the groovy girl if he could come, she had said, 'In your dreams.'

Usually, she'd just swear at him. He took it as an invitation.

If only he and Johnny Apeshit hadn't spent all their money on a fourth-hand two-track sound system, to record half-arsed demos, to give away at all the gigs they hadn't lined up yet. He couldn't ask his dad for any more dough, either. John Piero had just bought him a brand new bass drum and pedal.

To pay for the night he went down to the local mechanic's.

Steve Petrou was a good man. All solid and Greek. For five dollars an hour Bobby could clean engines and sand panels for him.

Bobby scrubbed, Bobby scrubbed, Bobby scrubbed, Bobby scrubbed, Bobby scrubbed, Bobby hosed, Bobby scrubbed, Bobby scrubbed, Bobby scrubbed, Bobby hosed, Bobby scrubbed, Bobby scrubbed, Bobby scrubbed, Bobby hosed, Bobby scrubbed, Bobby hosed, Bobby scrubbed, Bobby scrubbed, Bobby scrubbed, Bobby scrubbed, Bobby scrubbed, Bobby scrubbed, Bobby hosed.

The first hour went.

Bobby scrubbed, Bobby scrubbed, Bobby scrubbed, Bobby scrubbed, Bobby scrubbed, Bobby scrubbed, Bobby hosed, Bobby scrubbed, Bobby cut his finger, Bobby hosed, Bobby scrubbed, Bobby scrubbed, Bobby scrubbed, Bobby scrubbed, Bobby hosed. He started to not like Steve so much.

Bobby scrubbed, Bobby scrubbed, Bobby scrubbed, Bobby hosed, Bobby scrubbed, Bobby hosed.

The second hour went.

Ten dollars.
Two bourbon cans. Or. A small pizza. Or. One third of a CD.
Terrific.
Bobby sanded, Bobby sanded, Bobby sanded, Bobby sanded, Bobby sanded, Bobby sanded, Bobby sanded, Bobby sanded, Bobby sanded, Bobby sanded, Bobby sanded, Bobby sanded, Bobby sanded, one of Bobby's fingers started to bleed, he put a bandaid on it, Bobby sanded, Bobby sanded, Bobby sanded, Bobby sanded, Bobby sanded. He liked Steve even less. It was nothing personal. Bobby sanded, Bobby sanded.

The third hour went.

Fifteen dollars. Bobby could now afford a large pizza, or half a CD. *Stop it*, he thought. *Work maths will kill you!*
Bobby sanded, Bobby sanded, Bobby sanded, Bobby sanded, Bobby sanded, Bobby sanded, Bobby sanded, Bobby sanded, Bobby sanded, Bobby sanded, Bobby sanded, Bobby sanded, Bobby put another bandaid on, Bobby sanded, Bobby sanded, Bobby sanded, Steve was a bastard, nothing personal, Bobby sanded, Bobby sanded, Bobby sanded, finally, the first good song of the day came on the radio, a customer revved his engine so loud Bobby couldn't hear it.

Bobby sanded, Bobby sanded, Bobby sanded, Bobby sanded, Bobby sanded, Bobby sanded, Bobby sanded, Bobby washed the sanding back.

Lunch.

Bobby now knew about forever.

When Steve went to the shop, Bobby tried changing the radio station. One of the workers warned him against it, but Bobby didn't care. *Damn straight* music was worth getting the sack over.

'What is it about Greeks and their disco, anyway?' he mumbled to no one.

While Steve was gone, Bobby thought about the party. About groovy girls. He hated them, he loved them. So colourful, so far from him. So snobby. So scary. So sexy.

He thought about music. About playing it. A good mike for his drums would cost about $100. Twenty hours of scrubbing and sanding. Twenty hours! *God damn work maths!*

He changed his mind. Best not to think of music.

Steve came back from the tucker shop and changed the radio back to the disco station without blinking.

'Hey, nice try,' he said to every and anyone.

Bobby scrubbed, Bobby scrubbed, Bobby scrubbed, Bobby scrubbed, Bobby scrubbed, Bobby scrubbed, Bobby scrubbed, Bobby hosed, Bobby scrubbed, Bobby cut another one of his fingers, Bobby scrubbed, Bobby scrubbed, Bobby scrubbed, Bobby scrubbed, Bobby scrubbed, Bobby hated Steve. The man was helping him out. One of his machines could have done the job cheaper.

But he was still the enemy.

Bobby scrubbed, Bobby scrubbed, Bobby scrubbed, Bobby scrubbed, Bobby scrubbed, Bobby scrubbed, Bobby replaced a soggy bandaid, Bobby hosed, Bobby felt his life draining away, Bobby scrubbed, Bobby scrubbed.

His fifth hour went like years of a prison sentence.

Twenty-five dollars.

Still no sign of another good song on the radio.

Bobby scrubbed, Bobby hosed, Bobby scrubbed, Bobby scrubbed, Bobby scrubbed, Bobby scrubbed. Ten more minutes went. *That was, hm, ten minutes is one sixth of an hour, one sixth of $5 is, hm, is, hm, is . . .* Bobby slowed down.

'Hey, Bobby! Don't think!' Steve half joked.

'Oh. Sorry.' Bobby sped up again.

Bobby scrubbed, Bobby scrubbed, Bobby scrubbed, Bobby scrubbed, Bobby scrubbed, Bobby scrubbed, Bobby went to the toilet.

One sixth of $5 is. . . hm, I dunno! Something just under a dollar! I think. Half a Mars Bar. A quarter of a UDL can.

Just under a twentieth of a set of drumsticks.

Steve needed an errand run. He looked around but couldn't find Bobby. Suddenly, his toilet yelled, 'Aargh! Shut up work maths!'

'Hey, Bobby! Don't think!' Steve called to it.

'Sorry,' the toilet told him.

The only other good song of the day came on while Bobby was out on his errand.

32. Belief and Prayer

Sassy woke in a dark sandstone room. She had no idea how the Firebreakers did that. She would go to sleep, then wake in some place, in some mood, totally different.

Wherever she was, she felt this instant relief. An absence of pressure and smothering fright, that had been circling, more and more, back home.

She looked around.

The room's window had old, wooden shudders, but no glass. A view of other sandstone huts, a flat horizon, the slight fog of midnight plains. Everything lit by a deep, silver moon. Everything one cold, warming lunar tone.

No neon for a thousand, thousand kilometres.

'So easy,' she whispered.

Sassy stood by the window, watching the silent, chunky world. Somewhere in the city's background she heard a shrill, beautiful voice singing an Arabic call to prayer. It echoed through the lanes, huts, dust, shadows and moon.

'Where are we?' she said.

Mona eased into the moonlight, became a part of its silent, still, liquid tone.

'It doesn't matter,' her voice soothed beggars, rats and prison bars.

'Please. Where?'

'Somewhere where belief is strong.'

Sassy listened out the window for the man with his call to prayer. In the still of midnight and sandstone, it seemed to come from everywhere, be for everyone. To watch over and protect them.

It seemed, to her, like the most romantic of things.

'How did we get here?' Sassy whispered.

She remembered bits. Vague bits. Time was so strange with the Firebreakers. It went impossibly fast, it went impossibly slow. It followed no rules, no logic, other than music, atmospheres, moods. Moments that seemed to last forever, did. Time that seemed to drift by, drifted by. She had no idea how it worked. Not any of it.

'Does it matter?' Mona purred.

Sassy looked around. Matter or not, she was lost in a quiet, silver landscape. In another world.

'Come, child,' the jazz singer made her way to the roof. 'Clouds arrive.'

Mona stood on the roof, between Sassy and the moon, became a silhouette, with a powerful background of sharp clouds. Clouds that billowed, streaked, that reached, tucked, smudged, yet barely moved at all. That, lit as they were, seemed worth exploring, more solid, more real than the hazy earth below.

The man of prayers sang. His voice echoed. It believed in its God, in its world. When Sassy looked for him, all she could see were sandstone roofs and shadow.

'What do you want from us?' Mona asked. 'What is this *want*, child?'

'I . . .' Sassy thought about it, then knew better than to think. She just said. And waited, like Mona, on what her mouth told them.

'I . . . I don't know . . . I want to be lost. Not scared lost, not confused. Just lost. Just . . .'

Hard silver clouds gathered. Mists rose. Mona sang, soft, as though she was a backbeat to Sassy's words.

The man of prayers worshipped and wailed.

'I . . . I want to feel without reason. There's always reasons. I . . . I'm no good at them . . . I . . . I don't want them. To be lost . . . I want . . . Lost . . . Is . . . Is that so bad . . .?'

The man sang full of gentle, burning passion. Mona's voice fed off it.

She looked down at the child in front of her and smiled.

Sassy was offended at first. Pissed off. She had given Mona everything and Mona had just looked at her like she was stupid and small. She turned to leave, but to where? All she could see was sandstone and shadow. All she could hear was a wondrous call, thick in the still night air.

Maybe, whatever it was she wanted, this lostness she needed, was searching so hard for, maybe she was already there.

Sassy's mouth was out of words. Thinking hurt. She closed her eyes to hide from trying to explain what was impossible to explain.

Soon, she felt movement about her. Heard a wet, crumpled sound. Skin and blood flopping to the ground. There was an enormous weight somewhere close. In the air.

When she opened her eyes, the mists had risen to embrace the lunar sky.

Everything was tones. Everything.

And, in a night without distance, without time, there was a large, dark shape. Flame trickled out from where its mouth might be, thin, red licks dribbling up solid, black cheekbones.

The mist made it feel like a dream. Still, Sassy was afraid.

Eyes in the dark looked at her.

'You are not ready to see me yet,' it growled. 'Close your eyes again, child.'

Sassy did. And Mona's voice returned.

'This is occupied land,' the singer's voice explained. 'These people have nothing. They have had their homes taken from them, their running water, their fields, their land. There are tanks where streetlamps and markets had been. They have been given nothing but dust, rubble and fear.'

'I don't . . .' Sassy started.

'Shh . . .' Mona purred. 'What you are becoming isn't easy. There will be conflict. Always conflict . . . Listen, child . . .'

Sassy listened to the sweet echo of a sole voice, lost in the night. And, in listening, knew why Mona had taken her through the world to hear it. On tape, trapped in a CD, without its moment, its texture and power, it would have sounded like a grating yell to her. Nothing more.

This man, his voice, full of belief and yearning, to hear it as the sandstone huts did, it had such naked, indescribable beauty and power.

The man of prayers sang. He pushed rough grace and soft pride into the dreams of his troubled world.

'Music,' Mona's voice said. 'Music and prayer. Belief is the one thing they can't take away. They can build tanks to the moon. They can thunder like rabid dogs of fear. But they will never stop music or weather. Never control heat or rain. Never!'

Sassy felt flame.

'Music, weather, the oceans depths, the mind. They are the planet's last frontiers,' Mona breathed. 'And dragons, the few of us left, we are strong in them all.'

Sassy said nothing. Sassy listened to the call to prayer.

'Believe in music, child,' Mona's voice sighed. 'Make an ally of weather, like weather makes time its slave. Use it to fight fear.'

Sassy's eyes were still closed.

'I . . . I'm not sure I understand,' she confessed into the mist.

'Know that music makes you untouchable,' Mona's voice seemed to smile.

'Even the slaves sang, child . . . Even the slaves.'

Sassy said nothing.

She swayed to a beautiful voice she could never do justice to. Never explain. Not to her friends, not to her father. Not to Bobby.

Not to those not lost, not there.

Not to the other Firebreakers, not to herself.

She could just hear, just feel. Feel love. Without reason, without direction.

Just feel.

A heavy weight lifted from the roof, taking to lunar landscapes, to billowing, streaking, sliding midnight clouds. Clouds drenched in belief from the land below. This shape, it fed off, bathed and lost itself in, old world airs.

Sassy kept her eyes closed, her heart open, her hands spread wide.

She just listened, as a man, somewhere in a dark sandstone city, sang a beautiful, unfathomable song.

Just listened to a voice praying, calling to us all.

33. An Airless Man

The room was top heavy with pamphlets and still air. All four walls messy with tidy advice. Army brochures, career options, safe-sex fliers, drug warnings, activities sheets. Lectures on glossy paper.

In the middle of them all, fitting neatly, like set-squares and framework, was the guidance counsellor.

And Bobby.

He had no idea why. There were worse than him. He was a straight C student.

'Hmm . . .' the guidance counsellor looked at report cards. 'Does it bother you that your sister's so sick?' he asked.

'Sick?'

'We've just received a note from her doctor. She'll be going to a different school. Nearer the hospital. Surely you know that.'

'You're lying,' said Bobby.

But he knew the counsellor wasn't. Not deliberately. He was just dumb the way most people who think they know everything are dumb. If Sassy was cutting ties it had nothing to do with sickness or hospitals or different schools. Everything to do with jazz and things Other. What a way to hear it. From a guidance counsellor.

The man had caught Bobby on the back foot. Was ready to cram him full of his pamphlet advice.

But Bobby was onto it.

'Why's there no radio in here?' he shot quicker.

'Hm?'

'No music. You have your own office. That's, like, bonus points.'

'Music distracts me,' the man said.

And, like that, Bobby knew him.

He was the Enemy!

'Tell me about your mother?' the Enemy asked.

'She died,' said Bobby.

'I know.'

Bobby knew he knew. Knew the pamphlets knew. Knew the Enemy probably had files on it. Knew he probably knew more about what happened than Bobby. Every time his grades slipped, or shit happened, it was the same old question.

'Get over it,' Bobby told him.

'Excuse me?'

'You heard. Get over it.'

Pamphlets staggered back. The Enemy blinked. Tried again.

'When your mother died, how did you feel?'

'What do you care? Get over it.'

'I care,' insisted the Enemy, giving all his time-clock emotion. His concern by numbers.

Bobby just looked at him.

'It helps if you open up. You need —'

'Get over it.'

'I —'

'Get over it.'

Bobby and the Enemy glared at each other. The two of them sat in silence. Nothing moved. Not the pamphlets, not the guidance counsellor, not Bobby.

After three minutes, the Enemy said, 'You can go now.'

Bobby had dinner with his dad in awkward silence. They never talked about Sassy. Neither knew why.

When he was done, Bobby made his way past pale streetlights, through the smell of rust and dead lawns, to Falla's poster cave. Its leers, its sneers, its no-names, its legends. Each image to him — corny, bizarre, or cool — read like a pamphlet on Life.

Falla's dad opened the door, singlet and undies on, all stubble and crazy hair, eating something purple and grey from the fridge. The man was rough as guts.

Rough. As. Guts.

Too rough to care about noise. Too rough to care what neighbours thought.

'I'm here to practise,' Bobby said.

Falla's dad pouted. Raised his eyebrows up into his crazy hair. Every bit of him seemed to say *So what?*

'Doesn't it bug you?' Bobby almost protested. 'I mean, it's a work night.'

'You're having a go,' Falla's dad coughed, then went back to fall asleep in front of the TV again.

Bobby looked at Falla.

'One and a two and a . . .' he belted into it.

The two of them laughed and played and missed a great movie and, between songs, talked about any and everything.

'How come you never ask me about Mum?' Bobby asked.

'I dunno . . . Should I?' Falla scratched at his dark, rough skin.

'I mean, she died. What do they want me to say?'

'Dunno.'

'Me neither.'

Bobby and Falla said nothing for a while. It felt good. To have a friend you could say nothing to.

'Hey,' Falla lit up. 'I had a dream I was dead!'

'Yeah, what was it like?'

'Boring. I was dead. Everything was dark and worms ate me and I was dead.'

'Yeah, yeah. I get it. You were —'

'*Dead*,' Falla grinned, then laughed.

It was a great laugh.

Falla Jordan didn't give a fig about what happened before birth or after death. He'd deal with it then. Or not.

'Sorry about your mum,' he said.

'Yeah . . . well . . .' said Bobby.

When Bobby and Falla had talked themselves into dead ends, midnight hours and no more answers, they hit the music again. Lost themselves in it.

Just played and played until nothing mattered.

34. Sax and Horns

Summer came with a chest cold. It slowly warmed footpaths and tap water, but kept coughing up frosty nights.

John Piero was worried. Sassy hadn't been home for three weeks. He had no idea how to find her. Then, passing her room, he'd noticed an old photo of her mother. She'd coloured the face in black.

It was time to break that promise.

The one about trust.

Tracking her down wouldn't be easy. He thought about Mona. What she used to mean to him. How it affected him. But it had been too long.

He decided to get drunk.

John Piero swayed and wobbled under streetlights, like some hopeless, floppy thing. He stood in the middle of the road, bourbon bottle in hand, on drunken, sleeping feet, while his head, neck, belly and knees argued with each other about gravity.

Anger stopped his eyes from rolling. They were the only solid things his body owned.

He stood in the street, stared up at Raglus's side window, shouting all the obvious things.

'I know you're in there!' was one.

And:

'Come out and face me!'

He even gave that good old fight-picker a whirl.

'Oi! Wanker! Yeah, you! Wanker!'

A classic!

He'd never been good at one-liners and was too drunk to change now.

Cars eased their way around him as though he was a disease.

'Piss off!' they called.

'Get off the road, moron!'

'Go home, baldy!'

'Classics!' cried John Piero. 'The whole world's yelling classics!'

Then he noticed a policeman on foot patrol noticing him.

The man in deep navy blue uniform looked him over. Looked up past him, nodded and walked on. When John Piero wobbled his head back around, Mona had finally appeared in Raglus's window.

With Sassy behind her.

Mona said nothing at first. She was already taller than most plumbers. Already much taller than this stumpy, bald one. But, one storey up, she was plain intimidating.

Superb.

'You're drunk,' she finally spoke.

John Piero wobbled. Blinked.

'I have a lot to be drunk about,' he replied.

Mona looked down in hard silence.

'Who doesn't?' she said.

'First time in years,' John Piero waved his almost empty bottle at the jazz singer. 'I couldn't find you. I had to break down my logic. Become base.'

She said nothing.

'The air around you . . .' Sassy's father wobbled. 'It's . . . thicker.

It . . . feels. It's like this . . . beacon . . .'

'What do you want?' Mona asked.

There were others behind her, now. The whole band. A spurt of traffic hissed by. Someone honked and yelled.

'She shinks you're hur mother,' John Piero slurred, pointing an angry finger at Sassy.

'Is that all?' Mona said.

'*Is that all?!*' John Piero raged.

'What else do you want?'

'Else . . .? I want to be sure my daughter's safe. From —'

'I think there's more . . .' Mona cut him off as if he was barely there.

Then John Piero heard horns.

Drums and horns. Lots of horns. Mona stepped onto the landing and he heard sharp, twisting, falling, rising, almost musical noise.

The singer wore a long red dress, fleshed out by her smooth, dark-brown skin. He had interrupted something. They were on their way out. She looked all wrong, yet right, framed by the plumbing of dirty, plain apartment walls.

The band stood cold and hard. Nobody was playing anything. Not a note, not a beat. Yet the drums and horns increased, like wind, as Mona worked her way down the stairs. They rained and rolled and fell and approached in a violent chaos tide. Mona was chaos. Chaos!

All smooth and tired-eyed.

Under horns, under squawking saxophones and barging trombones and mad-arsed trumpets, Mona walked onto the street, easy, direct, towards John Piero as though she was a five-kilometre-per-hour freight train.

Then, over music and anarchy, she held his head in her palms. Looked down on him.

'I will show you something. Yourself through me,' she said. 'It will cost you a week.'

John Piero felt a jolt!

An incredible sensation of speed.

Weather rolled in like an avalanche. The moon head-butted the horizon, dawn vomited itself up. Morning peak hour rocketed past. As all this happened he felt himself go home alone, sleep, wake and join the shotgun of morning traffic in one swift, dipping motion. Then he spat out from peak hour into work, where everything was a blur of motion, muddy ditches and sweat. An argument about bonuses with the foreman before lunch took a blink to happen. He simmered with anger while he finished his day, which took five more blinks. Then he was hurling himself through the mad wash of peak hour again and from his window at home saw the sun hit the horizon like a comet and the sunset explode and fade as though it was a bomb that was running late. In a handful more seconds there was a mad scramble that must have been his dreams, before another dawn and day and night of his life fell and all John Piero could feel was speed. And all he could hear was the mad, awkward tumble of horns. And another day and night of his life passed. And the speed had a grip of him. And another day and night. Full bellies passed like hiccups. Hunger came and went like an indicator switch.

Then there was jazz. Passion. Music.

The music was timeless.

Timeless.

Timeless.

Then there was speed again. Another day of John Piero's life shot itself through the heart. Another half-dollar wage coughed into children and bills. In two blinks he'd fallen asleep in front of the TV. And another day passed. The crush of sensations, of speed and noise and falling, never let up. And through the chaos and horns the plumber reached for Mona's hands and ripped them from his head.

John Piero stood in the middle of the road. Sober. Sweating like a pig. Violently sucking in air, as though screaming in reverse.

Somehow, he'd aged a week. He could feel it.

'We live in different speeds,' Mona said. 'If we ever met, we met in music. I'm sorry I don't remember.'

John Piero dropped to all fours, to better suck in air.

Mona turned back to the fire-escape. Looked up at Sassy.

'I'm not your mother,' she said, as she walked. 'Your mother died.'

Sassy ran past Mona, to her father, to help him up. To hug him like need. To hug and hug and apologise and apologise and apologise.

And walk him to his home. *His* home. Not hers. Not anymore.

35. Mr Muir

Mr Muir was smug. He wore polo-neck jumpers and had this thing
for the class board. Bobby knew it. Everybody knew it. He would
come in and write on the thing as though it was a security blanket,
write any old stuff, even if he didn't have to. He'd just look at
the board and breathe and write, drawing strength from it until
he felt he could face the class without throwing up all
over them.

This day was no different.

He came in and wrote and everybody shut up and waited for
him to face them. It was a routine that told Bobby the whole day
would be a routine, so why not sleep for the next six hours with his
eyes open? Five minutes into the day, he kicked back, kicked his
brain loose and waited for school to finish.

Johnny Apeshit was there, trapped in Muir's silence. It was the
only class they had together. Bobby watched him doing nothing.
Thinking nothing. Waiting.

Then Falla arrived. Late, as always.

He stuck his head through the door. Saw Mr Muir writing on the
board, twenty kids facing front, quiet, obedient. They reminded him
of cattle.

'We might have a gig!' Falla mouthed to Bobby and Johnny
Apeshit.

Then, before Muir could turn around, he pulled his head back out the door, and let it stroll in with the rest of him.

A few of the class giggled. Not over anything Falla had done, but because he was sure to do something. Because he was Falla.

Mr Muir kept his eyes on the board.

'Office, Falla Jordan,' he said.

'Huh? What for?' Falla boomed.

'I don't know. For whatever you were going to do. I'm not in the mood. Just tell the Principal whatever it was, you did it.'

'Oh . . .' Falla stood there. 'Okay.'

He turned to face the class. Smirked.

'Don't do it,' Mr Muir insisted, tired before the morning was even up and running. 'Just go to the office. *Say* you did it. Call it a favour.'

'Did what?!'

'Don't you listen? Whatever it was you were going to do.'

Falla scratched. Looked at him.

'A favour?'

'I'll *owe* you one.'

Falla listened to the teacher's sarcastic tone. Looked at him again. At the class. They looked at him. A few of them blinked a bit. His smirk grew across his face the way a water balloon hits the pavement.

He couldn't help it.

'Moo,' he said to his fellow students.

Muir bit his tongue.

'Moo . . . o . . . oo,' Falla jutted the bottom of his jaw out.

'*Office!*'

'Mmmhrooohhh!' Falla bellowed, then laughed as he made an air guitar motion at Johnny.

'*A gig!*' he mouthed and headed for the Principal.

'Sir?' Bobby put his hand up.

'Yes, you can go to the office, too, Bobby Piero,' said Mr Muir.

'*A gig!*' Bobby mouthed at Johnny, then headed after Falla.

He half stopped at the door, as if remembering things.

'Oh, and "Moo", sir. Just to make it official.'

'*Out!*' Mr Muir raged, hanging onto his beloved board to stop from drowning.

Bobby left.

Mr Muir finally turned to face the class. 'John?' he pushed his eyebrows at the door.

'No, sir,' Johnny Apeshit told him.

'Are you sure?'

'Yeah. My dad would towel me. I'll catch up with them at recess.'

36. Doorways and Reptiles

Sassy and Maria stared at the tall man standing in the barber-shop entrance. The man stared back at Sassy. He had no lips she could see and wore a pin-stripe suit that, if it could, would cough dust and faded, black memories. He would have looked stupid, out of place, anywhere besides a run-down barber's doorway.

But that's where he was and he didn't look stupid. He looked mean. Frightening.

Sassy gripped Maria's arm. Poor Maria. They'd been catching up. Walking. She had said she wanted to know all about Sassy's new school, the one Bobby had mentioned, then, before Sassy could answer, started prattling on about the old one.

There Maria was — busy sounding like a pot lid, clanging, hissing and steaming away in the background — then this tall, skinny man had just, sort of, suddenly, been standing beside them.

'Do I know you?' Sassy said in her hardest voice.

'Do you?' the man raised half an eyebrow.

Sassy saw the snare drum under his arm, looked at the rot in his teeth, felt his bad intent.

'You're that man Bobby told me to watch out for. The busker. The Reptile, he called you.'

The man gave a smirk that made good moods pack up and move to other neighbourhoods.

'Do you understand Fate?' he hissed.

Sassy knew what the word meant. She said nothing.

'Who is this nut?' Maria whined.

The man ignored her.

'People with our . . . view of the world, can feel Fate. Like heat . . .' he hissed. 'There is a Gathering coming. I'm involved. Mona . . . You.'

'Me?'

'You. There's death. There's fire.'

'Shut up, creepo! Talk to the hand, baby!' Maria sneered. 'This sleaze is bad news, Sassy! Let's get out of here.'

'Who dies?' Sassy said, gripping her friend tighter.

'Who knows? But Fate is heating the air about us. And like moths to flame, they're coming.'

God, his voice, the way he talks, thought Sassy. *It's all rattlesnakes and sunburn.*

'Who's coming?'

'Don't you listen, child? A Gathering attracts them like flies to poo. Spectators. Tourists. Your friends. *My* friends. Atmospheres, temperatures, shadows. The Unsick. Rages and light-streams. The Swirl. Only a child couldn't see them.'

Sassy gave him a look without meaning to. Confused, annoyed, angry.

'My, my . . .' the man sucked in spit and air. 'Haven't your friends told you?'

'I . . .'

'Sassy, let go!' Maria punched at her grip.

'Here,' the man hissed. 'I'll show you what you're up against. Close your eyes.'

'What?'

'I can't show you with your little friend there. She doesn't believe. Your hunger for jazz and mystery is so passionate you'll believe in anything. That's why you're so easy to me. A little children's book. A dot to dot. I just go from A to B and *presto,* you're drawn and quartered. Close your eyes.'

'Hey!' Maria protested. 'Don't call me little, you freak-o-rama!' She couldn't understand why Sassy's grip was so unbreakable.

Sassy closed her eyes.

She could feel the street air, could hear the traffic. There was something standing in front of her. Some kind of pressure bearing down on her eyelids. A feeling of spite and fear, a knot of anger.

'Feel,' a voice came from its centre.

And Sassy felt that pressure grow. It rose like mountain faults, like earthquakes. It rose like history. Like blood. It rose like the world does when you fall from great heights. It screamed and growled and towered over her mind's eye.

That pressure, it gave off the stench of hate, it felt like nausea. Sassy was trapped by it. Totally.

Then a high-pitched scream made her open her eyes.

Sassy watched Maria's head dart left and right, as if trying to spot things in the corner of her eye.

She followed her friend's darting eyes, yet saw nothing. Just a street. But, when her own head turned, putting the busker in the corner of her eye, she heard punches. The most distant of voices swearing.

Panicked, she looked at the man. He stood there. Watching her. But now he was ruffled. His impossibly solid cheekbones, with their impossibly tight skin, were swollen.

Once more, she started to feel that pressure on her brain.

Something caught the corner of her eye again. She darted her head. Nothing. Just traffic. Watching it left the busker in the corner of her eye. She heard a flurry of blows.

She looked back.

The man was more ruffled. He had more fresh cuts and bruises. He stood tall. Stood hard, stood proud. Staring at Sassy, as if trying to re-engage her mind.

There was that pressure. Growing. Drowning her.

'Sassy!' a voice called.

It was Raglus. He was standing on the street corner, sweating with the effort it had taken him to rush there. Sassy looked at him waving his hands at her, placing the man in the doorway exactly in the corner of her eye again.

She heard blows rain, ripping and tearing sounds of the busker fighting back.

'No!' he yelled, furious. It sounded like he was thrashing wild. 'Girl! Watch! Over here!'

Sassy made to steal a glance. If only for fear.

'Kid, look at me!' Raglus pleaded.

Sassy kept her eyes locked onto Raglus as the world snapped and bent beside her.

'Keep looking,' he insisted.

The trumpeter kept his line of vision as he charged at Sassy and Maria, scooping them up and running them out of there.

37. Neither Are We

Maria hadn't seen anything. Not really. Just that Sassy was strong and wouldn't let go of her arm and was talking spastic to creepy men in doorways before something in the corner of her eye had frightened her.

'Your new school is bad news! Get a therapist,' she protested at the sudden weirdness of her friend, and stormed out of there.

It was dark in the pub. Cooling dark. Warming dark.

Relaxing.

'How handy are Blurs?' Raglus sighed.

Sassy said nothing.

It was midday. There was just Raglus, her, the barman. And CT Virus up on stage, practising.

Or so she thought.

Gradually, Sassy noticed there were a few other people in there. She could hear their small talk, but when she nervously turned to look at them, they were sitting still, silent, in shadows watching CT Virus. The harder she looked at them, the fuzzier their edges became, the more her eyes slid right off them.

Raglus watched Sassy. She was still terrified. Wound tighter than all the cold wars.

'They're not human, are they?' she demanded, motioning over her shoulder.

'Not really,' Raglus kicked back. He watched CT Virus, too. The clarinet player stopped and started again and practised.

'What *are* they, then?' Sassy demanded.

'Blurs? They're the things found in the corner of your eye, that make you turn your head when nobody's there. That make you think someone is in your house talking, before you realise it's just a tap dripping, or the coffee pot rattling,' Raglus's voice made it all easy.

'I still don't . . .' said Sassy. 'But, then . . .'

'Don't be so human, wanting every little detail. They're mysteries. Don't try to solve them. You'll unravel the poor bastards,' Raglus laughed. 'It would be like murder.'

'But, they . . . they helped. What do they get out of helping?'

'Well . . .' Raglus rolled his head, searching for one of those clicks your neck gives you. 'These ones aren't the ones who just helped us. But, as a rule, you can trust a Blur.'

'But what do they get out of —'

'Food,' Raglus said. 'We feed them.'

Okay. Enough was enough. Sassy didn't want to know any more about Blurs for the moment. It had already been a bad day. She had no desire to know what rotting things she was expected to feed half-real creatures.

'My God,' she suddenly said. 'The busker! That man, in the doorway!'

'Yeah?'

'He was so big. So dangerous!'

'Relax, kid,' Raglus said. 'He was just bluffing you. Showing you his presence.'

'But it was huge!'

'Sure. So's mine. And yours.'

'Mine . . .?' Sassy protested.

'Yeah, it's growing. Ask the Blurs, they're fascinated by it. You've a way to go yet, but why do you think that bloke is after us? Why do you think the Blurs agreed to watch over you? We're creatures of consequence.'

'After us?'

'Yep.'

'Watch over me?'

'Mm-hm. And your dad and brother. They fetched me to help you.'

'Creatures of consequence?'

'Right on.'

'Creatures? What, like . . .?'

'We're hunted,' CT Virus said from up on stage. 'Like trophies. We're trophies.'

'Creatures of consequence,' insisted Raglus, like a statement of lazy pride, rather than an admission of danger.

There was something about his voice. He should have rented it out. It could make the meanest of babies stop crying.

Sassy tried, Sassy tried, but Raglus was just too cruisy to be worked-up around. Somehow, he released her tension like slow leaks let down tyres.

'Come on,' he said, pulling his trumpet from behind the bar. 'This place will be open soon. Let's play.'

Raglus joined CT up on stage and practised. They started, stopped and started again. Hit bum notes, found brief, brilliant moments. Lost themselves, easy, in music.

It was all too much for Sassy, so she climbed up and sang along, as best she could. Went with Raglus's flow. Trusted him. And CT Virus. And even Blurs, whatever they were. She was in it now. In it with them.

Really, trust was her only option.

38. Rust and Dead Lawns

The neighbourhood smelt like rust.

It looked like rust. All the lawns were dry and cracked. Lawns didn't matter there. Water cost. Dogs weren't walked, they were owned. Dogs barked. That's what they were there for.

House paint cracked and peeled. Only cars had colour that wasn't faded, interiors that weren't secondhand. Bodies that weren't rust. Not every car, but enough. Enough to notice that, in this neighbourhood, a car meant a lot.

They would rumble by, slow and heavy, pounding an easy, throaty threat of strength, V8 motors and cranked-up stereos. Or sit in yards, over all those dead lawns, as if each one was a thousand football trophies melted into a set of wheels. Trophies chromed, polished and parked by bedroom windows with shotguns in them. Alarms would stop a thief, but not give you a crack at revenge.

Cars.

They took you to work at the factory to pay for your car. Took you to work at the 7-Eleven to pay for the car stereo. Took you to your mate's, the shopping strip, the pub, the dole office. Cars got you out of the house, stirred the still air. Took you nowhere and gave you motion. Helped you *feel* like you were on the move.

Cars were freedom. Pure and simple.

Cars.

You couldn't change the world, not here, but you could rebuild a motor, no worries. Achieve your bog-job goals.

Only the things that mattered, mattered in Falla's neighbourhood. Bobby loved the place. He loved its cars. They held a language. A language to know, be good at.

They were music.

To people around here, anyway.

Bobby, Falla and Johnny Apeshit wanted to play music that was simple and gutsy.

That sounded good in cars.

Falla's dad had four or five old Holdens. None of them were worth two bob. He liked taking them apart, but wasn't good enough to put them together again. A bit here, a bit there, he was sure that in amongst it all was one good *Beast* that would somehow build itself by morning.

The three boys kicked back in the sun, chassis and car parts of the front yard. They listened to music from the poster cave, argued, soaked up heat and bad tempers off the dead lawn.

Bobby could feel something watching him. Sometimes he heard voices, lost in the background noise of the day. Some kind of distant echo of his sister and her life, no doubt. It creeped him out. But his band made him feel solid. At least they were there, in front of him.

Pissing and moaning.

Johnny Apeshit put on his best caveman voice.

'Duh. We might have a gig!'

Falla laughed without emotion. 'Funny,' he let the word fall out of his mouth like a dead, rotting thing, then threw it, with a look, at Johnny's feet.

Maybe it was the heat, but Johnny wouldn't let up.

'Duh. A gig!' He clunked around as if he was a gorilla playing air guitar.

'Yeah, well we might!'

It made no sense, Johnny and Bobby knew it. Falla had found out there was some bloke living across the road who owned a pub with a dingy, little band room. That was it.

He hadn't talked to him, hadn't even seen the man. Yet there Falla was, at school, playing air guitar, raising false hopes.

So someone from the piss-trough end of the music scene lived on Falla's block? So what? He was probably one of the neighbours who pounded on their wall whenever they practised.

'His name's Ronnie Wicks,' Falla said.

'How do you know?' Bobby asked.

'I stole his phone bill,' Falla said.

He pulled a letter out from his back pocket, held it up, laughed.

Johnny was lost in rust and heat. Narky.

'A gig!' he did the gorilla thing.

Falla threw a car part at him.

'I'll coconut you,' Apeshit spat.

'Don't you dare, white boy,' Falla growled.

'I mean it.'

'Don't you bloody dare!'

'Dark on the outside,' he pinched at Falla's brown skin, 'white on the insi —'

Falla threw another car part, hard.

'Here it comes,' Johnny chimed.

Falla glared.

The two of them stared at each other.

'White boy . . .' whispered Falla.

They stared.

'. . . coconut . . .' said Johnny.

And it was on.

They launched and hit hard, raising rust and dead grass. Falla, bigger, solider, worked his way on top, covered Johnny's face with his hand and pushed it hard, into the mangy, dead lawn.

'Cocon —' Johnny started through dark fingers.

Falla pushed harder. Dogs barked. Johnny kicked Falla in the back, drove his fingers into Falla's nose and mouth. He switched it around.

Falla's head hit the ground hard. Smothered under hands and arms and elbows, he winced. Half laughed. Breathed hard.

Johnny kept up the pressure.

Dogs barked, dogs barked.

'Hnuh. Your mum's . . . poor . . . white trash,' Falla grunted through pink fingers.

Both of them put in. They thrashed and wrestled and pulled free. Stood, glaring at each other, holding gravel burns, sucking in rust and car parts.

Then they noticed Bobby, about to knock on Ronnie Wicks' fly-wire door.

39. Mud

Sassy stood on the hill behind the lot, watching her father, down in the mud. He dug trenches, laid pipes. Covered himself with slop and sweat. Earned a small, honest wage.

He worked.

And Sassy watched as the site foreman came and went, looking down and shouting at him.

'Come on, Piero! For hell's sake!'

'I . . .'

'The cement truck is on the clock. Your wage is paying for it!'

'Tricky bit. More rock than . . .'

'I don't want to hear it.'

Sassy had met some of his bosses. There were good ones, bad ones. This one knew John Piero was hopeless with paperwork, so he disputed everything. Work time, equipment costs, money owed.

She watched her father shovel, while the pink cement truck idled around the front, waiting to bury his work. John Piero liked being a plumber. He was a physical man. Some of the contracts were good, honest.

But this job site had no music in it.

'Hi,' Sassy said to her dad.

John Piero looked up through the mud, saw his daughter's flowing hair.

'Honey!' he lit up.

Sassy smiled a dopey smile.

'How's school?' John Piero asked.

Sassy let the wind wash her hair over her face. Shrugged from somewhere behind it.

'Oh. How's the other stuff?' the plumber tried to keep his tone up, keep his child happy. 'How's jazz?'

Sassy gave double dopey smiles.

John Piero looked over her shoulder for his boss. Started shovelling again, just in case.

'I used to do magic tricks for your mum, you know?'

'Sure . . .' Sassy doubted.

'True! I once gave her three moonrises in a night.'

'As if, Dad!'

'True!'

'Yeah, how?' she said, as though she knew things he didn't.

'Well, I had an old FX Holden back then. A great rust bucket. We packed a midnight lunch and I took her up to the hills near the water catchment above town. And we, like, watched this beautiful moonrise over the distant plains. It lit the thin fog, made the small hills look like, I don't know, solid, black waves.'

'What shape was the moon?'

John Piero shovelled, but didn't really shovel at all.

'Oh, full,' he said, as if he would only give the best. 'The moon was still rising, so as I drove your mum back down the hills, it was swallowed by their height.'

'I'm onto it, Dad.' Sassy grinned.

'We settled and snogged . . .'

'Dad . . .!'

'. . . and watched it rise through the trees from a valley bridge. Then we cruised back into the city's heart, where it got lost in the bustle of buildings, and we watched it rise over skyscrapers, from a café!'

Sassy beamed.

'One night, three moonrises. Magic!' John Piero insisted, smiling like the muddy little frog that ate all the flies.

Then more abuse thundered from somewhere within the lunch hut.

'Piero! You'd better be done soon! Or else!'

'Listen, Dad, I didn't . . . actually come here . . . to see you.'

'Oh.'

'But, um, you were close . . . and it was great to see you . . . I, um, gotta go . . .'

John Piero shovelled hard.

'See you tonight?' he asked. There was a father's need in his voice.

Sassy had things to do. There was a trapdoor CT Virus wanted her to explore.

'We can watch some TV, play cards . . .' her father asked more.

'. . . Sure,' his daughter smiled.

'PI-BLOODY-ERO!' the boss raged.

And Sassy was gone.

Sassy *had* come to see her dad, but, watching and listening, her head had pounded, her heart had raged.

She slipped into the lunch hut, so her father couldn't see. Walked up to the site foreman, who was eating a pie in front of a newspaper. Her blood crashed, her blood boomed. It thumped and bashed as if trying to thrash free of pink skin walls.

'Why don't you ever pay him the bonuses you promise?' she asked.

Bass drums rumbled.

'Hey, who are you, kid?' the boss chewed.

Sassy's blood surged. Cats fought, mothers cried. Empty train tracks moaned.

'Why didn't you just order the cement truck an hour later? Why don't you help? Or just sack him?'

The man looked. She was just a small, annoying girl. Pow. Straight from nowhere. But there was something about her. A rising storm and pain.

Sassy's insides boiled, her bones screamed. That damn pulse of hers filled her ears. She couldn't hear herself over its thumping beat, but spoke anyway.

'I'm going to hurt you now,' her mouth said.

The foreman blinked once. Blinked twice.

'Why . . .?' he heard himself ask.

Sassy's head was swirling with things not right, with madness and jazz. She felt the man's garlic and sweat, the fear seeping from his pores.

'Because John Piero's my father,' she growled.

40. Ronnie Wicks
(and dog)

Ronnie Wicks had a small dog. It stood between his ankles. It yapped.

It yap, yap, yap, ran in a circle, yapped.

'Man!' Falla said.

Ronnie didn't seem to hear it. He watched the boys through his fly-wire.

'. . . *Let me guess, you want a gig?*' he said. He had a fast, clipped way of talking, like a used car salesman who didn't want you to hear the fine print.

He was a tall, skinny man, with a skinny voice, tight jeans and a big, fat hair-do.

'Your pub's gutsy,' Bobby told him.

Ronnie looked at them more. His dog yap, yap, yapped.

'*Sure. Why do you want to be in music?*' he rattled and stopped.

'Hey. A quiz!' Falla laughed.

'Women,' Johnny shouted over the yapping.

'Because,' said Bobby. 'Just because.'

Falla liked that one. He nodded his head at Bobby like cartoons.

'*You know there's no money in it, don't you?*' Ronnie rattled and stopped.

'Wow,' Johnny said. 'Um. Are you my father?'

'No money?' Falla sooked. Then laughed.

The dog yapped, scared itself with a fart, scurried behind Ronnie's legs, then yapped at its arse.

All three boys just, sorta, watched it as it scurried, farted and yapped in little circles.

'*What do you call your band?*' Ronnie rattled and stopped. Damn he spoke fast!

'Whaddo you mean?' said Falla.

'Who cares?' twitched Johnny.

'Something, I guess,' Bobby told him.

The dog yapped.

'*Well, which is it?*'

'I don't give a shit!' Johnny Apeshit finally lost it. Everyone could see it was only a matter of time before he dropped to all fours and started yapping back.

Ronnie laughed on the inside.

They don't even care about a cool name, he thought. *They just want to play.*

His brain worked like his mouth. Short and sharp. Rattle and stop.

They're money for jam, it thought.

'*Okay,*' he said. '*Sundaysareemptyinthebandroom.Onegigamonth. YoucanhireaP.A.fromme.Thenthere'smikes,stagehire,thedoorgirl. Lighting,GST,insurance.Lookingatyou,Ithinkitmightbebestifyouwork offtheexpensescleaningformeandhavethedoortakingsfor yourselves.Keepitsimple.Youcanstartwithdiggingupmybackyard tomorrow.Obviouslyyouaren'toldenoughtobeinthere.I'mtakingachance withyou,sodon'tblowit.*'

The dog yapped.

Bobby, Falla and Johnny stood there blinking like rabbits in headlights. Ronnie watched their mouths open and close as they tried to understand what he'd just told them.

'. . . A gig?' Falla finally said.

'*Now piss off*,' Ronnie Wicks waved them out of there.

The boys were feeling good. They kicked back, easy, in the car parts, cranked the stereo. Threw loud, raw songs out the poster-cave window, as though the world was their lounge and the music was *their* dog barking.

'Free labour!' Bobby protested.

'Dodgy,' Falla agreed.

'Kill that dog . . .' Johnny grumbled.

'The way he talked . . .!'

'Aren't the mikes supplied by the venue, anyway? And what the hell is stage hire . . .?'

'Throw some rat poison over the fence . . .'

'Ripped off.'

'Blind.'

'Or go in commando-style . . .'

'A gig!' grinned Bobby.

41. Hungry Fingers

The lights were on in Raglus's flat. Everything was back-to-front jazz posters and plain, white walls.

Sassy and Mona watched Palestine playing bass.

Bass did nothing for Sassy. Not for her ears. But watching Palestine play was something else.

His fingers ran smooth and precise. They ran, they ran, they ran. His head was lost in the sounds they made — eyes closed, chin down, sweet, simple, lost. It looked like his whole body was deferring to his fingers. Humbled by them.

His fingers, they ran, and his heart followed.

Sassy felt safe watching him. Safe enough to ask: 'Mona, this hunger? This hunger for music, to be good at it?'

'Yes, child.'

'What happens if I achieve what I want? What happens to the hunger?'

Mona watched Palestine as his fingers strode through a wide, curving patch of sound.

'You are right, child. Palestine's fingers are running,' she said.

Damn it! Sassy hated the way Mona would steal into her thoughts like that.

'Only your musical thoughts, child. I can feel them. In your body language. They burn.'

Damn it, again!

'They're running,' Mona nodded at Palestine's hands. 'Full of that hunger you talk of. And will always be running. If you are in love with something, not just passing through it, the hunger never leaves.'

'Like my father loved you?'

Mona regarded Sassy.

'Like he loved your mother.'

Palestine's fingers slowed. They thumped, slid and pressed, held and rang some notes dry. His eyes stayed closed, his head stayed down. Who knew what his fingers were running him from? Or to? What dragon tales, or sorrow or madness?

'But my hunger's so strong, it hurts. Sometimes it hurts real bad,' Sassy pleaded.

'Oh yes, child,' Mona purred.

42. Brood

The Reptile sat in darkness, brooding, as insects and strange things skittered around him. Slowly, over days, over weeks, shadows had gathered. Dropped off, like hitchhikers, by the night.

He liked the railway yards. They were the city's heart, reaching out like veins to all the meanness in the suburbs. They had gravel and steel and no people at night. He sat in a cream-coloured portable hut, in his grey overalls and yellow reflector vest, surrounded by rust-coloured freight carriages. No paint, no gardens, no decoration for miles. Just plumbing like tree roots, working its random way down, through nooks and crevices, into and along the ground. Just signals and cables and generators and flour mills. Every inch built as it was needed, nothing for the way it looked.

Everything just man-made nature.

He listened to the cockroaches, felt for arrivals. Played his snare drum, soft and easy.

That snare drum, it sent out messages along railway lines, along bluestone rocks and steel and humming power boxes. Messages that ran to things living in garbage and sorrow. That fill the cobwebs of abandoned stations, that haunt bleak, fading shopping strips.

He played and he hated.

He hated, and each rap, each steel brush slide, filled him with

153

spite until it oozed from ears and old wounds. Until that hate filled his calling.

He drew in bad vibes, called on rumours, heartache, things that trip people when their hands are full, and voices that whisper, 'Go for it . . .' in your ear, but only lead to car accidents.

He dipped into poor neighbourhoods, into conctrete backyards, caged birds and all things stagnant. He romanced every hurt, every bitterness.

He called, he hated.

The Reptile rapped out a slow, venomous beat. If one in every one hundred answered his call, he'd have all the shades he needed.

He despised every one of them. Wanted to rip, to tear and cut them. But he had bigger wants, bigger challenges.

Mona, the Firebreakers.

After all these years of waiting for a weak link in the Firebreakers, along came the girl. Now, thanks to her, he had an in.

Now, thanks to him, the Gathering was coming.

Suddenly, light swept across the portable hut. A security guard stepped out of his car, waded through the freight carriages, shone his torch through the window. Its iron bars made neat, bright squares all over the Reptile.

Keys jangled.

The man was fat and ordinary.

'Hey, what are you doing here?' he said to the person sitting in front of him.

'Overtime.'

One bloke in overalls was much the same as another to the security guard. There was nothing in any of these joints worth stealing. Graffiti and vandalism, the homeless, were his only concern.

'Geez, at least turn on the light, will you?' he moaned.

The security guard flicked the switch. For a second everything

was blinding. The Reptile winced, but didn't move. The security guard
made his way to the sink, with a sigh, to make a coffee.

There was a click. A flash of piercing white light.

He spun to see two men behind the Reptile. They wore press
cards and cameras around their necks. Had fresh money in their
pockets. The taller one was rewinding. The room otherwise empty.

'Who the hell are *they*?' the security guard whined.

'Freelance photographers,' the Reptile said, without emotion.

'I don't like people taking my photo. What if I'd blinked?' the
security guard complained. 'What is it with photos, anyway? Why take
my photo?'

The Reptile mimicked him. Pushed his bottom lip into a sooky
little jabba-jabba.

'Well,' he wiped a trickle of pus from his earlobe, 'if you had
been mythical, he would have just killed you.'

'What a kook!' the security guard grumbled to himself, as he
squeezed back into his car. 'All types in this job! All types.'

Bright lights swept back across the hut as he pushed on to other
yards, other warehouses, to find other blokes in overalls to whine
and complain to, wondering all the while how he ended up in a job
so lonely.

One of the press switched off the light.

Shadows refilled themselves.

The Reptile's shiny, pale skin took in the cold. He rapped out his
beat, not loud, not hurried. A million insects made their way to him.

There was so much to look forward to.

43. Fold-out Bed

Everything was a whirl, a thousand drains swirling with a million colours.

Sassy lay on the fold-out bed in Jodi's one-bedroom house, stared at nothing and felt her blood changing. Less and less of her body felt like the small girl who looked back at her from the mirror. She tried to read a book, but the words blurred. She couldn't focus.

It had been happening a lot lately.

It must be these late nights, she thought as she watched the sunrise seep into the old, grey wooden fence out the window.

At ten to seven one of the neighbour's radio alarms went off. Sassy listened as a DJ crackled, bubbled, popped and tried to kid his listeners that the cold, dull morning was really a party, so why not get up anyway.

After all, that was his job. To be happy and enthusiastic about getting up for you. To be your energy when you had none.

Sassy tried to picture a world with morning DJs who were grumpy. She laughed to herself. It wouldn't take much to inspire students to become rebels, or convince factory workers and secretaries to go out there and clobber their bosses and demand more money. Or not show up at all.

'*God, the whole city would collapse!*' Sassy whispered with a chuckle.

As seven o'clock approached, Sassy heard another alarm go off. And another. It rained beeps and buzzes and bouncing DJs.

The alarms all tried to make a run for it, but were slapped, thumped and flicked off by their owners.

Wait for it, thought Sassy.

Sure enough, nine minutes later, snooze buttons kicked in all over the neighbourhood. Alarms and buzzers and DJs went off again, and morning's race was off and fumbling and tired-eyed and running.

Sassy fell asleep. At last.

And dreamed.

The world was browns and greys and greens, the colours of soil and rocks and trees.

Sassy went to read a book, but its pages were all empty. And another. Empty. She walked through the browns and greys and greens to an endless row of books and looked at a few, and knew they were all empty.

Bored and frustrated, she went to a movie.

The cinema had light mists, an atmosphere of earth colours. Sassy could hear the film, but the screen was empty.

When she walked back out into the street the billboards were empty. The newspapers: empty.

She felt cut off. Had this great, big, desperate need to talk to someone. To connect. But everyone on the street, under brown and grey and green sky, was reading, or watching TVs through windows, or looking at their digital watches.

Everybody, all her friends, the life she knew, seemed flat, cardboard.

Then some of the earth colours shaped themselves into jazz.

Sweet jazz.

Sassy turned and there was Mona, and she was brown and grey and green and had this neon energy. And looked like a story.

A powerful story. And the trees were a story. And the old Italian man who worked at the fish'n'chip shop who always told tales of his past was a story.

And the music, it flowed greens. It flowed greys. It flowed browns.

It flowed earth and neon.

It flowed reds and purples and whites and yellows and held emotion. Emotion in which she could plant her stories. Stories that flowed, like bark.

But the music stopped. The jazz stopped.

And Sassy felt like she was drowning in browns and greys and greens and cardboard.

She knew that newspapers were okay and books were fun and movies were the coolest, but she just couldn't grasp them.

She tried desperately to find that music again. To be safe in it.

Sassy grabbed through the earth colours for its song sheet.

But the pages were empty.

Sassy felt her blood changing. She sang. She sang and sang, to protect herself from becoming cardboard.

Sassy woke around midday.

Sat bolt upright.

Jodi was awake, her small portable TV coughing and sputtering to itself in the corner. The solid Chinese woman did the dishes, listened to the idiot box, but never watched the thing.

Sassy listened. *The Jerry Springer Show* was on. She smiled. Sassy loved Jerry Springer! She thought of the show as a modern colosseum. Some dickheads would come on and fight and the audience would cheer or boo with their thumbs up or down and the dickheads would go back home, to wherever they lived, away from the TV cameras, to be worshipped or beheaded.

Sassy moved to the edge of her bed to try to see which clowns were on today, but found it hard to focus on the images.

Suddenly, she knew why jazz was so important to the Firebreakers. Not just for its passion. The blues had passion. Rock had passion.

Jazz, their type of jazz, flowed. Had no music sheets.

Was improvised.

'No wonder you're hunted . . . Dragons, you're like cats and dogs, your eyes aren't complex enough. You can't see things that are two-dimensional. You're not human. Not at all,' she said to Jodi. 'Palestine was right. You're animals.'

Jodi gave and dropped a smile and went back to doing the dishes.

Sassy sat on the end of her fold-out bed. Sat and listened to Jerry Springer and felt her blood changing.

44. Big Night Out

The song had stopped. Well, Bobby and Johnny had. Falla strummed and wailed away, lost under his hair, until Bobby threw a drumstick at him.

The room echoed. The place was as good as empty.

'We need more friends,' Falla said into the microphone.

A man sitting to the side stood and walked out. The barman was doubled over, laughing his guts out. The only other person in the room was a drunk at the back.

'Hey, there!' Falla said through his hair.

The man seemed to either roar, or dry heave. Either way it was pretty scary.

'Sorry,' Falla said.

The doorgirl chewed her gum as though she had something against it. She hated no-name bands. That meant no crowd. No crowd meant no one to treat like shit. Treating people like shit was her thing. Her status.

'Get on with it!' she spat.

The barman waited, wide-eyed for the next song.

'A one and . . .' Falla said, then suddenly started hammering away at his guitar. He turned and laughed at the other two, as they scrambled to catch up.

Johnny Apeshit's guitar thrashed as though it was trying to buck free of him. Falla sang the lines he remembered, yelled 'Walla, walla, walla!' over those he'd forgotten, threw his chest at invisible walls. Bobby fell from his milk crate, hollered like a madman, belting at the ground until his feet took him back within hitting distance of his drums again.

A few people came, then went. The band played. Bobby thumped and thumped with all the guts he could muster.

Push it, he thought. *Push it forward . . .*

Eventually, the drunk threw up. The barman yelled at him. The place was still empty. Bobby pounded out an intro beat.

'Hey. Someone else is leaving,' Falla cut him off.

Bobby and Johnny lifted their heads to see a pretty girl. She'd only just walked in, but was about to leave again. To look for a room with other pretty people. A room with a juke box, not a band, so all their attention could be on each other and how pretty they were.

Falla turned a stagelight towards her.

'Where are you going?' he said into the mike.

Pinned by the light, the pretty girl murmured something, pointing vaguely to the main bar.

'Oh. The toilet,' Falla said. 'That's okay . . . We'll wait . . .'

They stood there for half a second, waiting, and laughed, and Johnny Apeshit absolutely ripped into it.

He crashed into his guitar, letting its sound arch and fall towards the start of a song, like the moment when a roller-coaster pushes over its tallest peek.

The three of them braced themselves for impact, filled their ribs with anger. When Johnny's guitar slid down, smacking into ground zero, they exploded into raw music.

No one was watching. Bobby brassed it out. But everything felt hollow.

Then three people made their way to the band room door from

the smoke and noise of the public bar. The doorgirl, now in full spite mode, tried to talk them out of coming in.

'Do you mind?' Falla said mid-song.

The band played as the people made their way to the back, bought drinks and cheered and yelled and shook and went with it. Went with all of it. The music, the volume, the sound, the anger.

The three paying customers hopped right on the band's volume train, and, within a song, turned the empty room into a bloody victory.

Falla roared at them. They roared back. Everybody stood there, under music and pub lights, roaring at each other. The room seemed to heat up. Fires flared all over the city.

Drums and cymbals bashed and crashed around Bobby's face. He caught glimpses of the three people dancing. Stagelights made it hard, but he saw a goatee beard. A solid . . . maybe Asian . . . woman? A skinny dude, spiky hair.

The lighting shifted and strobed and seemed to make the walls dance. Falla busted guitar strings but didn't give a damn. Johnny kept tripping on his lead. Bobby made to thump his cymbal into orbit, but missed and hit his knee.

When the song finished, the barman crawled onto the stage in tears to shake their hands.

Eventually, the door girl packed up. More people came and left with free entry. A few stuck around and talked and didn't care.

The band played all six songs they knew, then, knowing they weren't good enough to play them the same way twice, played them again.

A few more bodies strolled in. But, really, the place was still empty.

Bobby belted and raged. Buried himself in sound. He was in trouble. They all were. All that work shot in an hour. Money gone, money gone. Pissed into the wind.

At least those three people at the back were loving it.

At least that was something.

The boys stepped off the stage covered in sweat. The crowd of seven or eight joined the public bar's crush of smoke and beer talk. Only the barman stayed. He wiped his tears away and smiled and hugged the boys as though he knew things about hopelessness and insanity.

Ronnie Wicks gave them their door takings while they were packing up. $20. Divided into three. One and a bit hours less of sanding for Steve Petrou.

The boys had enough gardening and cleaning to cover two more shows, crowd or no crowd.

But Ronnie was sacking them.

'But who's going to fill our spot?' Johnny protested.

'*Ah. A band of uni kids,*' he rattled and stopped. '*They've got uni mates, so there should be a few more through the door. They can do a little work for me like you did.*'

Falla mouthed what Ronnie had just told them.

'. . . Are they better than us?' he finally asked.

Ronnie Wicks hadn't even heard them. He said nothing in a way that made it clear Falla's question was nothing.

Money was money.

'But . . .' said Johnny. 'You owe us . . .'

Ronnie just gave them more hard looks. Business was business. Music was business.

Then, for the first time in his life, Bobby yelled at someone. Really yelled. Gave it all his blood and venom.

'You're the goddamn Enemy!'

'The Enemy!' Bobby yelled again as the security threw them out on their heads and elbows.

Bobby, Johnny Apeshit and Falla stood in the middle of a busy night street. Headlights, tail-lights, taxis and kebab shops everywhere.

'Shiite,' Falla kicked at his guitar. Its last string went twang. It was an improvement.

'Screw him!' Johnny Apeshit shouted.

Scambling to gather his drum kit, everybody gawking, suddenly Bobby felt good. Furious and great, all pissed off and sensational.

It seemed the simplest thing to be ripped off. To have no crowd. To be all stupid and doing it. He was the oily rag other people drove off.

Besides, for a moment there had been a moment. Raw power! Yelling and music. Three people and a barman loving it.

He hated Ronnie Wicks with all the guts his guts could muster. But nobody died.

They went back to Falla's to piss and moan and celebrate.

45. Black Vinyl

John Piero watched a vinyl record spin for the first time in
twelve years.

It span, slow, on his turntable, a round black hole in his empty,
unlit lounge. It made him feel dated, prehistoric, left over from the
old days, as if he were tin toys or milk bottles.

The record had no label. It turned and turned and no sound
came out. Soon, it crackled and spat and the crackling and spitting
made the silence even sweeter. John Piero looked into it until
it became not just a hole in his lounge, but a pit. Until the softly
spinning grooves surrounded him, and his heart fell inside its slow,
rotating vortex.

Everything was round and black in John Piero's mind.

Everything was silence, crackle and spit.

Then he could hear the murmur of a crowd. Then a trumpet.

Then a distant voice sang.

A voice almost drowned by the rustling sound of the jacket that
had hidden the recording equipment. A voice almost lost under the
crowd. A voice peppered by the crackle and spit of black vinyl.

A woman's voice. Passionate, full of power.

Eventually, John Piero reached for a photo of his wife. He gave
it a kiss full of love and duty. Full of the gentle emotions.

He stared into the photo, as if he could meet its eyes.

'Help me, love. What do I do?' he asked it.

In the background jazz spat, jazz crackled, jazz played, a dark woman's voice called to all things that burn, to all weathers.

'I . . . I . . . What do I do . . .?' John Piero repeated. 'I want to save my daughter and I want to be her.'

46. Stress, Syrup and Mush

A year had passed.

Christmas seemed to sneak up on the city and smack it around the ears. In a blink the streets were coated with thick layers of heat, stress, syrup and mush.

Good people loved, let it all hang out. Bastards pretended they cared. Money was spent.

Bobby gave his father just one present. A beauty. He told his dad to get off the couch. Turn off the tube. Stand still. And gave him a three minute hug, all real and neverending. He even sealed it with a small slapping drum beat on the old man's back.

Good stuff! Job done.

His kid sister had one coming. A hug to squeeze her dodgy socks off. But Sassy wasn't there. Wasn't anywhere.

'Enough's enough,' he growled to no one.

Bobby screeched to a halt at the feet of the One Man Carnival, dust and wrappers still billowing in his wake. Heads turned, birds bolted. In-store Santas hid under their beards.

Everything was collision courses and last prayers.

'Where is she?' Bobby said.

'THAT'S RIGHT, FOLKS! MOVIES! MOVIES, MOVIES, MOVIES!' the One Man Carnival coughed up chunks of volume.

'Where is she?' insisted Bobby.

The One Man Carnival stole a nervous glance.

'THAT'S RIGHT, FOLKS! POPCORN! POPCORN, POPCORN, POPCORN!'

'*Where is my sister?!*' Bobby yelled.

Traffic swerved to dodge his rage. A policeman turned his head. Criminals behaved. Somewhere in the background a busker stopped playing.

Everywhere, ears tuned in. Bobby could *feel* them.

So what.

The fat, noisy man in front of Bobby was a doorway. He knew it. Just being near him helped you become aware of things. Of people and places Bobby hated. Scary, strange things a sane person would run like all hell from.

But right now he wanted in. Nothing clever. No waiting, no listening for clues.

Just in.

'Where's my —'

'*OVERPRICED?!* I WON'T HEAR OF IT!' the One Man Carnival stole glances. 'WHY EACH INDIVIDUAL POPCORN IS HAND-CRAFTED, HAND PAINTED TO LOOK LIKE IT HAS BUTTER ON IT!'

'Hey, you! Yeah, you! Mr Hook-Nose . . .!'

'THAT SQUEAK IT MAKES WHEN YOU CHEW IT? DO YOU KNOW HOW HARD IT IS TO PUT THAT SQUEAK IN?'

'I mean it!'

'THERE AIN'T *NOTHING* LIKE OUR POPCORN!'

The fat man's mouth continued to hit the street, but his eyes were as busy as battery hens. They darted as if grabbing for someone, then slamdunked themselves hard, between each sentence, on top of Bobby's angry head.

'WE EVEN HAVE MOVIES TO GO WITH YOUR POPCORN! HOW GOOD IS THAT?!'

Grab, slam. Grab, slam.

'*Listen, I'm not going anywhere until –*' Bobby roared, then, yelped.

He felt himself being dragged away from the One Man Carnival by his ear. Hard, sharp pain blinded him. The hand that held Bobby was strong.

'Hey . . .!' he yelled. 'Hey . . .! Somebody . . .! Help . . .!'

'Shut up,' the hand's owner growled. It was a good growl. Mean enough to make the Devil pull his head in.

Bobby shut up.

Whoever had him marched on, at pace, mumbling, cursing.

'Of all the stupid . . . If not for . . . How bloody . . . Stupid . . . Open . . . Right out in the . . . *Stupid . . .!*'

Everything was a haze. All Bobby could see through his pain was a colour that wasn't sea-green, wasn't murky blue. That just wasn't. It felt more like an atmosphere, all even and deep and flat and neverending.

The man with the strong hand kept such a hard pace, they seemed to catch a wind. A wind that blew into a howling gale.

Bobby's ear marched on. He continued to scrape and scamper after it.

Enough was enough. He held the arm hard, did a chin-up on it. Looked sideways, up the nose of a policeman.

'Oh.'

'Hey, copper . . .' Bobby grunted.

The policeman said nothing, looked over his shoulder. More and more, he looked over his shoulder. Gradually, Bobby could hear the sound of busking. The steely rap of a drum. Feet, many feet skittering behind them.

'No, really, copper . . . My ear . . .'

Suddenly, the policeman span, shouting as he lurched hard.

Bobby felt an impact, then found himself flipping through the not sea-green, not murky blue . . .

Bobby slept, Bobby dreamed. His ears dreamed.

Everything was dark and warm. There was a party in the distance. Bobby could hear voices, could feel music. Jazz. But it was all too far away. Over there.

In Bobby's dream, he felt himself being argued over, decided upon. There was a fight of some kind. Ripping, tearing, impossible sounds. Hissing, a great roar. Hollow, echoing drum beats. Blood.

Cymbals and mad, scrambling jazz guitars.

Eventually, there was just a policeman's hard breath.

Soon, motion returned with sweet, flowing, approaching music. The party was with him now. Only it wasn't a party. It was what? A pub? A tavern? A memory?

A mood?

No, that was impossible. How could he be in a mood? *Am I awake or not?* Bobby thought to himself.

'Yeah, I'll take him home,' a lazy hammock said to a strong policeman's hand.

'Tell her to tell him!' the hand demanded.

'Yeah, sure,' the hammock replied.

47. Suburbia

It was late. Beyond that, Sassy had no idea of time. Not anymore.

Raglus sat on the small, concrete steps of a small suburban backyard. The streets smelled that grassy, treeless, suburban smell. The air held that distant, still suburban sound.

The trumpeter smiled.

'How did you find me?' his sharp, grinning teeth showed.

'CT.'

'Why?'

'I couldn't breathe. CT was playing this really cool jazz record, all crazy, like machine guns, and there was all this music and music and music and I just had to get away.'

'Isn't music what it's about?'

Sassy looked around.

'I'm . . . I just had to get some . . . space . . . and . . .' she reached. 'On the way here, behind every streetlight, I could hear this . . . noiseless shuffle . . . fighting . . . Shadows and Blurs . . . It sounds stupid but . . .'

'The Gathering.'

'It's like they're . . . I don't know . . .'

'Jostling for front-row seats. Picking sides.'

'Yes!'

'It makes you scared.'

'. . . Yes.'

'But that's not why you left CT's.'

'No,' Sassy bounced.

Raglus could hear hurt in her voice. He said nothing, if only to show her he was all ears.

Sassy, in turn, waited for the right words to form. They would trip and bubble out in no order, as always. But so what? Raglus carried ways. Simple, small ways. He had become her friend.

She knew if she had one thing around him, it was time.

A silence-packed forever later, she heard her voice say:

'I'm lonely.'

The trumpeter said nothing.

'I mean, music, jazz, gives me such . . . *Such victories!* Such strength and . . . and power and . . . *Such* . . . But when there isn't any music or I'm sick of it and can't . . . And there's no . . . I . . . Why can't my friends . . .? Why can't they feel like . . .? Burn like . . .?'

The trumpeter just grinned.

'And you and the others, you're all so . . . large and . . .'

Sassy looked up from her fumbling hands. Straight into Raglus's green eyes.

'How old are you?' she asked.

'That's none of your business, Sass.'

'Any of you?'

'Well, Palestine met Jesus,' he said.

Sassy spun without spinning. Surely he was putting her on.

'The carpenter,' Raglus added. 'Once. At a market. Says he was just this super-nice, honest bloke fronting an obscure little religious cult. Simple morals and a toga. Look now.'

'Raglus!' Sassy held onto some railing. 'My old friends don't . . . I miss them, but . . . Yet you're all so . . . And . . .'

Raglus watched Sassy as she shook with frustration and hopelessness.

He leaned forward and hugged her as if to say nothing was everything and everything was fine.

'Sass, there's a strength in wanting to be good. In loving something. Nothing's for nothing, though.'

'But . . .'

'Some music's about pushing boundaries, out past our abilities, past ourselves. Our music, it's, it's a living thing. No one song played the same way twice . . .'

'. . . I . . .'

'It's like . . . like sometimes you've got to live and play beyond everyone. Be alone . . . But when all that work and loneliness, when the crowd hears it as moods and easy sounds . . .'

'. . . It's all gold . . .' Sassy said in the smallest voice.

'It's all gold!' Raglus roared.

'But you and the Firebreakers have each other and I'm . . . I'm not yet . . .'

Sassy noticed someone standing behind her. She could feel a presence, dark and smooth.

'What are you doing here?' Mona growled.

Sassy turned to see the jazz singer in silk, denim and brown. Palestine and Jodi stood behind her. None of them happy.

'Wilson's my friend,' Raglus said. 'I'm visiting.'

Sassy quickly realised whatever they were here for was pureblood business. Animal protocol. Raglus, the half-breed, wasn't welcome. Not at all.

'So? Are you leaving?' Mona said.

She sounded so mean.

'I thought you could use a passenger,' Raglus told her.

Mona said nothing. Just stared at the trumpeter. Hard.

'You would be too heavy,' she finally lied.

'Not me,' he fired right back, all Raglus lazy. But underneath pulsed a strength Sassy never knew he had. The ginger-haired half-breed would stand up to volcanoes, win or lose, for the right cause.

'She's swimming against tides,' he said.

Mona suddenly realised there was a tiny girl in front of her. She looked at Sassy, smelt the air for unspoken questions, read her body language, felt for the weight of her need.

Raglus didn't have to say another thing.

'Then swim with them, child,' the singer's voice drifted down.

48. Guitar

The fly-wire door opened and closed with the thwack of all good, cheap fly-wire doors. Jodi, Palestine and Mona walked through Wilson's hall.

'Oh,yeah. And see to your brother when you get the chance! He's at home, and he . . .' Raglus's voice faded away.

Sassy followed the others, listening to the musician as he played his acoustic guitar. It sounded like the sweetest thing. All heavy, full of bass and strong fingernails.

One hand trickled and gripped all over the guitar's neck, gentle and strong. Pressing chords, playing sounds. The other strummed and picked, easing out a rich rolling sound. Not a note ended. They faded, long and slow, into other moods, into echoes. Towards horizons that would lead to islands full of stories if you could follow.

His two hands seemed to make three songs. Songs that weaved into and around, over and under each other.

Sassy watched the tall, ugly man. He was more solid than overweight, his clothes were loose, his heart was wide. She could feel it. Knew it. He sat on the edge of his bed, practising, playing, hunched over his instrument, pouring all his scars and dents into it, all his flesh and stories and soul.

He flowed, the room flowed. Crowd or no crowd.

'Hey, kid,' he said in a soft drawl. 'Good to see you . . .'

It was the first time they'd met, but his voice made Sassy feel that if she was hungry he'd be happy for her to take his whole fridge. Just because.

'I . . . Good to see you . . .' she replied.

Wilson's music grew and grew and he began to sing in that impossibly deep voice he owned. It poured into and around his three falling songs.

Sassy closed her eyes.

And listened.

And drifted without time.

Lost in song, Sassy now knew why music sounded better at night. Why people shut their eyes to sing their favourite, most hurtful lines. Why they don't keep them open to kiss. Why the yummiest food and a back rub and soaking up the sun and the moment of victory are best met with a moment of dark.

It makes something singular. Everything.

Physical.

Gradually, the coldest wind blew through Wilson's music, chilling Sassy to the bone.

Salty spray hit her face. An enormous, tumbling roar slid under the guitar. Time and distance refound themselves. Suddenly Sassy was aware she wasn't in suburbia anymore.

Neither were the purebloods.

She could feel them around her, in the howling midnight winds of Arctic waters, as a monstrous wave shattered deep seabeds in front of her, and another one behind them rose.

Sassy felt herself rise with it. The raft beneath her climbed through the dark, on hundreds of tonnes of moving water.

She rose one house high.

Two houses high.

Three.

The muscle of the wave was unbelievable. Gigantic. Prehistoric. It felt like death and madness. But within its avalanche, within its intent, Sassy could almost hear Wilson's song. Something so soft and flowing within something so violent and raw.

There were sharks and coral and bones within the black void beneath her. She rose and rose and peaked and knew there was no force stronger on earth than an angry sea. And knew, with Wilson's song in her heart, it wasn't ugly, but more brilliant than she could ever describe.

The wave collapsed in on itself in screaming wind and crushing motion. Sassy heard ripping and tearing as she fell head-on towards its impact, knew that three beasts fell with and around her, attacking, being one with the world and all its power.

Sassy fell.

And as she did, she could just hear one of the beasts, over the deafening roar, purr in her ear;

'Feast, child.'

49. It's Okay, Bro

Bobby woke slow. Tried to rid himself of sleep like a spoon tries to shake off honey.

He found himself in his bed, in the dark of his room.

All the elements of his dream were there. Outside, in the furthermost corner of his ear, a café kitchen-hand had been given ten minutes out from his sink to rock customers with his jazz guitar. Beyond that, a policeman cleaned up after a car accident, taking statements from the car owners, who had shouted and fought. Somewhere in the background Bobby could make out the murmur of a Christmas party, in which a lazy hammock-filled voice got up to make a ham-stacked speech.

Sassy stood on the fire-escape, layered in shadow.

'Sis?' Bobby squinted.

'It's okay, bro,' she told him. 'It didn't happen. Not really. They made it a dream.'

'What happened?' Bobby said.

Already his memories of strong policemen's hands, of flipping through the air, and colours that weren't, were doing what dreams do. Were fading.

'That greeny . . . it, like, wasn't . . .' Bobby's voice trailed off. 'That wind...' his hand rubbed his ear, his head clutched at sand.

No. Real or a dream, it was all fading.

Gone.

Only the fact of a missing afternoon remained. Bobby felt strange, dirty with things Other.

'Weird,' he said to himself.

'I know. How trippy is it?' Sassy beamed.

'It's not real, Sass. This thing you're doing.'

'What do you mean?'

'These things. All of it. It's not real.'

'Sure it is.'

'No it's not,' Bobby insisted.

Sassy lost it. As much as she could with someone she loved.

'*Your* life isn't real! It's . . .!' she started, before thinking better of it. 'Stop bringing mine down!'

'Sorry, Sass. It's just . . . Dad and it's Christmas and you didn't even —'

'I've seen him.' Sassy cut her brother off, her voice carried by soft applause and jazz guitars.

'But Dad. You didn't even . . .'

'I've *seen* him. Just before. While you were sleeping.'

'Still . . .' Bobby tried.

Then the truth came out. It wasn't about John Piero.

'We had a bond,' Bobby finally said with hard eyes. 'Never leave the other behind.'

For a moment, neither brother or sister spoke. Jazz guitar wove silky, faded cobwebs between buildings and lanes.

'I know,' Sassy threw out a hopeless guilty plea.

There was a wide, dark, deafening silence between them. A silence between best friends, that didn't need words.

A silence in which Sassy knew Bobby had not left her behind when he'd first heard that jazz, on that hot, smothering, red coal night. That Bobby, even though he hated jazz, had not left her behind when he had found that audition tavern down Spillane Lane.

She knew he never left her behind, not when he snuck her into the football, not when he went roaming the night, or walking in fat summer rain. Not ever.

Bobby stared.

He looked right into his kid sister, with strength and hurt. Looked with eyes that said you didn't need anything if you had family.

He didn't even have to repeat himself. His eyes, his silence, spoke for him.

Never leave the other behind.

'I know . . .' Sassy hurt. 'It's just that . . . You don't even like . . . You don't . . . Jazz . . . You haven't . . . I can't . . . You're so young and . . .'

Sassy started, Sassy started.

But she was no good at explaining herself. Not ever.

The words fell, tripped, died and Sassy ran away. Ran into the night and its background noise. Ran into thin, distant creamy layers of jazz guitar, dodgy buskers and traffic.

Bobby put a thumping track on. Filled his room like a thunderbox.

He moved to the window under hard drums and bone-naked guitars. Watched his kid sister go. Looked at all those strange creatures, half blurred and jerky, gathering, swirling around her, talking with her, as she slowed to a walk. He felt their smoke and power.

Sassy's brother loved her. Even if she was missing the point. It had nothing to do with jazz. Or even music.

Not to him.

Bobby Piero decided it didn't take two to be loyal. He whispered to the street.

'I'll watch out for you, anyway.'

50. Innocent

John Piero watched Sassy sleep.

It felt strange to have her home. It felt beautiful, it felt sad.

Dinner had been awkward. So had TV. Sassy didn't even seem to watch it. She just sat in front of the thing, letting her vision roam, as if doing favours. As if acting out old times.

The silences had been awkward.

She'd given nothing away. Not told him what she'd been doing, where she'd been, why she was home for the night, why her clothes smelled like danger and romance. And he hadn't been brave enough to ask.

Now she slept.

Now she looked peaceful, like the child he'd raised. Like the innocent, young daughter he loved. John Piero stood by his baby, watching her sleep, as if watching was enough.

Soon, he noticed a tape had fallen out of her jacket pocket. He flicked it into her tape deck and listened, volume down low.

The first voice he heard was Sassy's, talking aimlessly, somewhere near a mike. Then he heard CT, then Raglus. He heard Mona cough and tried to stop his heart from speeding up.
The whole band was there, chatting, while one of them tuned an instrument.

Then Sassy mumbled 'okay' as she grabbed the mike.

'The Anger Song,' she said into it, with what sounded like a sheepish grin.

And began to sing.

And stopped. And began, and stumbled over a few lines, and worked her way into rhythm and lost it and stopped.

It was a practice tape, recorded for Sassy to hear how her voice did or didn't work.

'I . . . I'm not good at . . . Don't normally . . . Anger . . .' her voice wandered around the background.

The other band members talked to her.

She grabbed the mike again.

'This time . . .' she said into it, with sheepish grit.

And, from the quiet speakers of a small tape deck, Sassy's voice sang.

Scatting wasn't easy. Rambling as if you were a musical instrument without notes or plans. Looping sounds, creating a rhythm, a tune, a mood the whole band could slide along, with nothing more than words.

John Piero was impressed with how she rarely repeated herself, as most ordinary scatters did. Her mind must have been racing furiously, two lines ahead of her mouth, three lines ahead of the song. Finding the right phrases to suit her story, to push it forward. Words that fit the right dips and curves.

John Piero listened as her tongue tangled. The band waited for a four-beat and she started again.

Sassy sung up a fine mood. Her voice had been right, it was an anger song. John Piero lost himself in its flow. He felt mad, he raged, he grooved.

Gradually, he opened his ears to the words, to her song and her life, and felt shocked and felt dirty and felt amazed. He felt lost. Lost in her anger.

The song picked up a notch.

And again.

Sassy's voice grew in power, in confidence. The band played, the band played. John Piero's emotion grew with every word. He stood, watching his daughter sleep, tapping his fingers, clenching his teeth, riding with the quiet volume of a furious tune.

Then he was distracted by a car horn from the street below.

It was nothing, but when John Piero turned back to the tape deck, the song's spell had been broken. He heard his daughter's voice for what it was. For what it had shifted into with song.

Suddenly it growled.

Suddenly it snapped and tore and bit and had no words, just animal sounds. It was as if it never had any words. As if it had always been animal sounds.

It ran ahead of the music like a wolf leads a pack. Sounded guttural and mean, as if it was screaming for future and past revenge.

Tears swelling in his eyes, John Piero pressed Stop. Hands shaking, he slid the tape back into Sassy's jacket pocket.

Every bit of him shaking now, he watched his beautiful, innocent daughter sleeping as though at peace with the world.

51. 2 a.m.

All Bobby could see was the brass of cymbals and the white of drum skins.

He hammered, harder and harder.

Falla was inside, watching a video clip of skinheads singing a macho rap song. 'White wannabe-black, white supremists,' he had laughed at them.

Johnny wasn't there.

Bobby hammered.

The song he was playing had dropped off long ago. Nothing was left of it except white and brass and volume.

Sweat and rage.

The cymbals hissed and hissed and hissed and Bobby just kept hitting them. Something was going on. Something he hated.

Just thinking about it made him bash and thump and roll out all his violence and energy. If only to hide himself in his music's real world.

Those things in the corner of his eye, in the edges of his ear, they were everywhere. They were fretting. These shadows, they were being stalked by shadows . . . something.

Something, something, something.

Bobby thought about his drop-dead stupid thoughts and bashed and bashed, and bashed, furious with himself that they should be in his head at all. Brass fizzed and spat and crashed around his eyes, sticks blurred and pounded and fell.

Bobby could hear half voices, lost in his sound. Could almost see shapes in the dark of the room, beyond cymbals and drums. His arms charged at his skins like horse hooves and bombs. He picked his favourite song and, bashing and crashing, yelled the words.

But that dodgy, sinking feeling, in his anger and noise, just found more room to move.

Bobby turned it up. Gave it the lot. All he had. Everything. But it wasn't enough.

He knew it

Finally, he kicked his bass drum away, punched his snare. bowled over his cymbals and threw his sticks at the wall.

He cleared Falla's garage by throwing his instrument at things that weren't there. He did no good at all.

Bobby stood in the dark, sweating, breathing hard.

There was a new, old album he wanted to listen to. A bad music video or fifty he wanted to watch and complain about. A girl he wanted to chase. A song he wanted to learn.

But he had other things he had to do.

52. Truck Stop

Raglus had lost his driving licence. Something to do with demerit points. With flat things like traffic lights and stop signs. His friend Wilson was doing the driving for him.

The pair of them, Sassy and Palestine sat in a truck-stop window.

It was one of those stripped bare places, whose colour was dust. No CD box, no radio. No Blurs. Just the shuffle of feet. A cheap doorbell that sounded more like a short, sharp complaint. The downsizing of gears and hiss of hydraulic breaks. The buzz of truckie talk. Everything, every sound, honest, hard. Simple.

Each noise joined to become a whole. Music of sorts. Of truck drivers and till girls.

That's what they were there for, less obvious music. For Sassy.

But invisible tunes didn't matter at the moment. Not at all. Word had come through, via the trucks and their CBs, the blue-collar press.

Somewhere in the city they'd captured a dragon.

The trucks hissed, growled and grunted to themselves and each other. They stopped and started, fuelled up, unsettled the dust, added soot and grime. The drivers laughed at the news and half believed and didn't believe and didn't really care.

Sassy, Raglus and Palestine sat in noisy silence, hoping against what they'd overheard.

'It's true. It's CT,' said Wilson, making his way back from the pay phone. 'Mona tried. They won't post bail.'

Nobody said anything.

The coffee machine kept on clearing its throat. The doorbell punched itself, giving the till girl her 527th headache of the day. The dust swirled but didn't go anywhere.

'There's police, press, cameras, guards,' Wilson finally added. 'You won't get in there.'

Sassy looked around. Palestine was seething. A thin layer of smoke rose from behind his sunglasses, declaring holy war on the ceiling. He had to get out of there.

Palestine rose. Stood at the table, framed by truck-stop nowhere.

'You know where to find me,' he said to Raglus, then marched out into cold, grey daylight.

As he walked, the wind swirled dust from the bowser driveway, up under his jacket, through his hair. Then he was gone.

Not anywhere.

53. Stormy Weather

The weather coughed and sputtered all the way back to the city.

Sassy could feel the drizzle, its draughts and shifting mood.

The car had no tape deck. No radio. Just the flow of bitumen, the beat of broken white lines. The hiss of wind through jaded door seals, the slight vibration of a poor wheel alignment.

Sassy couldn't figure it out. Was it her new, weird blood? Or what the Firebreakers were teaching her? Any time, anywhere, even in truck stops, even now, in trouble and silence, she could hear music.

A simple, bopping tune of an old, worried car.

Wilson pulled in to the shoebox truck stop of an express-post town for more dust and fuel. More trucks and tired, stocky drivers. Blue singlets, blue singlets. The uniform of those too tough to wear uniforms.

Raglus bought a paper, hot off the press, full of cold facts. Wilson read it to them.

Some 'passing photographers' had captured footage of police stumbling across what looked like a mugging, but might have been a drunken fight. A young local jazz player had been jumped by an unknown busker.

The two-dimensional images were fuzzy to Sassy. She focused

as hard as she could. There were a few photos of the jazz player fighting. Another from outside the police station. All three pictures clearly showing hard, sharp teeth, lumpy skin and scales where his shirt had been ripped off him.

'They've even got his name,' Wilson read aloud. *'Held for questioning. CT Virus.'*

'And the busker?' asked Sassy.

'It says he got away.'

When they turned to get back in the car, Raglus was gone.

Wilson turned the key. The drizzle had strengthened. The wipers weren't working in tandem. They bumped and kissed and did their own awkward, clumsy thing. Their beat had a soft, bass tone to them.

It reminded Sassy of Palestine.

54. Black Honeycomb Crush

Wilson and Sassy pushed back into the city's burrowing heart. To its black honeycomb crush of bricks, concrete and people. To its views that went up, not along. To its grime, traffic and police stations.

To *the* police station, the one that held CT Virus.

The cops didn't know or care. They wouldn't let anyone see CT until 'the forensics boys' were done with him.

'Go home,' they said. 'Go on.'

So Sassy did, before they asked who *she* was. She didn't want forensics anywhere near her. She left Wilson to argue with all those men in blue acting so much like grey brick walls and went to Raglus's flat. Jodi was there, sitting by her drums.

'Where are the others?' they both asked at once.

Sassy and Jodi paced around the flat. Waited. Did nothing. There was nothing to be done.

By nightfall, a cold wind blew through the fire-escape window. It pushed behind all the jazz posters, making them do mad little belly dances.

'The cool change,' said Sassy. 'It's caught up from the highway.'

Jodi stuck her head out into the chilly wind, soaking it up, as if washing herself with it. As if listening for its history, its tales of mystery.

Meanwhile, Sassy listened to the latest news on the television.

'HOAX!' screamed one station.

'FAKE FOOTAGE! BLOOD TEST CONFUSION!' raged another.

'EARLY SAMPLES NOW PROVEN NORMAL!'

'It's too late,' Jodi whispered to no one, eyes closed, face lost in weather.

'What?' asked Sassy.

'Their disbelief. They're making him human . . .'

55. Oh . . .

It was strange.

The press said CT had been released. But to where? Sassy didn't know and couldn't ask. Everybody had gone. Even Jodi. Sassy had turned from the TV and she wasn't there.

Left alone, Sassy felt like the storm was tugging at her. She could feel things in her veins. Dragon rage, human hopelessness, small-girl worry. The silence was screaming, her mind raced with doubts, fear, worst case scenarios. She couldn't stay in the flat. Not a second longer.

Pushing through the empty night streets, the rain and green neon, she walked up to the one person who might still help her . . .

The One Man Carnival stood over Sassy, all round and hard angled. The two of them waited in the dark, as sharp rain roamed the streets. Cold and wet, they watched from across the lane, through CT's small window . . .

Outside his room the storm's wind howled. It pushed at walls, raised roofs, cut off power. It flooded gutters, ripped apart plants that had at first praised its coming. It made stop signs rattle with loneliness, left powerlines wailing sad stories to each other. It emptied streets. It filled them with water. It bled and howled.

And drove CT mad.

The clarinet player still looked the same. Thin, handsome. Strong.

But he paced his room, turned things over. Stared at the ceiling, the walls.

Looking closer, through the wet window, Sassy could see those long, thin, skeleton fingers of his twitching and jerking, as though trying to spell 'scared' time and again in the air. They kept grip, grip, gripping at his clarinet, as if it was a cell bar.

'I don't —' Sassy started.

The One Man Carnival put his finger to his lips, kept his eyes on the window. The flat box of white light in the middle of a dark, wet wall, in the middle of a shadowy, wet three-dimensional city.

CT paced, raged at his ceiling.

'I DON'T WANT YOUR PITY!' he bellowed. 'I. DON'T. WANT. YOUR. PITY! LEAVE ME ALONE! ALONE!'

His neighbours banged on floors and walls. Yelled at him to shut up. But all their protests, and CT's, were swept up and lost in the sound of the rain.

Sassy was shaking, and it wasn't just the cold.

Why was CT screaming at nothing? He seemed like a bird with its wings broken, scratching and flopping in little circles on the pavement while nobody stopped or cared. A magical creature who, due to human thinking, a nasty lack of faith, had been unplugged from the world.

'Come on, kid,' the One Man Carnival said. 'Let's leave.'

'But . . . he looks so lost . . .' Sassy pleaded, rain running down her neck, soaking her clothes. 'Shouldn't we —'

'You can't help him,' said the One Man Carnival. 'He's dead.'

'Dead . . .?'

'Look. Look hard. He is dead, like me.'

Sassy looked even closer. CT's skin was white, smooth. It had no lumps anymore. He'd been made human. Given a death sentence of old age. A prison of flesh, of clothes and walls. A death-throe of forty or so short, long years.

'The sky has been taken away from him,' the One Man Carnival said. 'They have infected him with the Yearning.'

'The Yearning . . .?' Sassy watched CT.

'For what was, and can never be,' said the spruiker. 'For the mystery he was. For his lost ability to feel the earth's pulse. To be the smoke and flesh of a myth.'

Sassy looked up at the One Man Carnival.

The storm filled water tanks, drowned animals, fed trees and wrecked lives. The rain hit her tears before they could even be called tears. Washed them to nothing.

Dead. Like me, he had said.

Suddenly she knew why he helped, but wouldn't talk about it. Why he never got too involved and shouted and shouted and always shouted and tried not to think and didn't sleep.

He was scared of memories. Of dreams. He was once something magic, something impossible and timeless. Immortal. And every time he helped her, or Bobby, or the Firebreakers, it reminded him that his soul had died and his body would soon follow.

'But . . .'

She was lost for words.

Now the One Man Carnival seemed hollow himself. Strong and empty. Hard and sad.

'But, CT . . . the Firebreakers? Why don't the Firebreakers help him, or comfort him, or something?' Sassy pleaded with all her heart.

'They are. They're saying farewell,' the One Man Carnival said over the howling wind.

'But where are they? They should be here!' Sassy cried.

'Pay attention,' the One Man Carnival pointed at his ears and eyes as he turned to leave.

Sassy was so cold her shoulders hurt. She focused through the hard rain, to watch CT one more time.

'LEAVE ME ALONE!' he twitched, jerked and paced. 'I DON'T WANT YOUR PITY! STOP REMINDING ME! STOP REMINDING ME!' he yelled over and over at the ceiling, as though it wasn't there, as though he was shouting at the clouds.

Then Sassy realised.

Mona, her band, they *were* the storm.

And the wind, the rain and thunder, the howling power cables, the property damage and million rattling windows, were all the Firebreakers' fault. Their cold, raw love pouring down on everything. They were singing a goodbye.

A eulogy.

56. Bobby and the Busker

The busker sat back in a portable hut. A railway-yard lunchroom. He wore overalls and work boots and smoked as though it was the easiest and worst thing in the world.

'Well, well, well,' he smirked. 'The Ears.'

Bobby said nothing.

'Do you know why things are going so wrong . . .?' the Reptile slid his words out. 'Why your sister's in so much trouble?'

Bobby said nothing.

'Your ears.'

Bobby said nothing.

'It's *your* fault,' insisted the Reptile.

Bobby remembered the first time he'd heard the Firebreakers all that long, short time ago. How, in hearing them, he and Sassy had gone looking. How he'd always listened to the silence, ever since he was a kid and he'd sit on the roof of the flats on hot summer nights and his dad would teach him how to play *Listen For That Tune*. They would put their ears out there, find noises in the silence. Separate them into garbage and music. Separate the music into home stereos and passing car radios and distant pub bands and lonely buskers. Separate the rock from the hip hop from the pop from the ballads. And his dad would give him bonus points for rare sounds like jazz.

It was a fun game, a good game. But they'd stopped playing it while he was still young, when his mum had died.

Bobby remembered how, ten years later, that game had shaped into a lazy habit. A habit that had sent his ears out into hot nights and, somehow, found cool dragons and dragged all this trouble home.

'Shit happens,' he said, and believed it.

The snare-drum busker was the problem in front of him.

'How did you find me?' the Reptile smoked.

'I can't explain it,' Bobby said. 'You have an echo. A not-at-all-right echo. Like you're calling to things. I followed it.'

'Why?'

'I've figured your secret,' Bobby told him.

The Reptile butted out as though grinding fingernails into blackboards. He took his time, he took his time.

'Which is?'

'You hate the Firebreakers for spite. I think you play your snare drum to help you get in rhythm with their music and, through that, their world, but . . . You're the sort of person who likes pulling things down, just to be an arsehole. You hate them because you aren't magic. You're not a Reptile, or whatever. Sure, you've learned tricks and stuff . . .'

'Get on with it!' the busker snapped.

'. . . but you're human. You hunt them because they're magic and you're only human.'

The Reptile sat in his seat, unmoving. Thick strips of smoke made ugly, grey layers of the hut's air.

'You're just a spiteful, common, railways maintenance worker,' Bobby said. 'I'm not scared of a railways maintenance worker.'

The Reptile leaned further back in his seat, as though he was wax, all sticky and hot. Head tilted back, he stared at Bobby. Figured things.

Then he darted across the portable hut at impossible speed.

His nicotine-stained hand clasped over Bobby's mouth and squeezed until Bobby's head was bursting to pop.

'Ah, but those tricks and stuff I've learned . . .' the Reptile hissed, 'are nasty and superb.'

57. Cockroach

It began with the sound of a cockroach.

A sound too small, too trivial, for any person to hear. But Palestine was no person. He half turned his ear from the Firebreakers and their circle of small talk.

No. It was nothing.

But the cockroach continued to skitter. Skitter in time.

Then, there was a drip from somewhere below. A drain? Some plumbing? It was so small. Just a drip.

Palestine turned. Listened. The drip almost had a rhythm to it.

No. It was too quiet. Too far. He couldn't tell.

The Firebreakers stood in harsh gym light, telling tales of crimson hurt, of blood red music and electric purple atmospheres.

A moth found its way into the gym. It thrashed at the green exit sign. It bashed and thumped, dived and headbutted, pounded. Up there. Five metres from anybody.

The Firebreakers continued to talk. Waiting for Jodi to finish work and get there. Sassy laughed.

The moth kept snaring Palestine's ear. He concentrated over his shoulder. He listened, he listened.

The moth attacked the exit sign. Bashed and bashed and bashed itself against green plastic.

To a beat.

A drum-beat.

Palestine listened.

The cockroach crawled, insects moved. They slithered, hopped, in hot summer night — as they did everywhere — but they had rhythm about them. Palestine was almost sure of it, now.

He listened to sounds way beneath sounds. To tickles and trickles. The drip kept on. The moth hit and hit and hit. He could feel shadows slither in the dark. Caught a vague whiff of something in the warm, night air.

The smell of fear.

'Firebreakers,' he cut through their laughter. 'The Gathering is here.'

Then, as the band turned, the gym doors exploded forward.

And there was noise. A horrible, dark avalanche of noise.

The rage of car wrecks, the crawling madness of envy. The power of guns. The volume of the press. The thunder of rage!

There was the busker in his pinstripe suit, bleached yellow by time. A man who looked mean, like a Reptile, with a snare drum around his waist, throwing a small boy through the air.

The Firebreakers watched as Bobby whooshed past them, into the drum kit at the far end of the gym floor.

58. White Sound, White Heat

There was a wall of sound. There was no sound.

Bobby tried to yell, but nothing came out.

There was a swirl. A maddening, bizarre, black and white swirl, a storm of shapes moving around the Reptile. Bobby watched through a swollen eye as the busker walked forward through blurred shapes that fought and reached through living shadows. Shapes that seemed to almost grab at him, only to burn and die in Bobby's vision.

If they were real, if they could scream, their screams were matched, by this raging, piercing wail of misery and heartache. It came from the dark. From insects. From railway lines. From blotches in unlit doors and windows.

Sound became violent and sharp. Hotter and hotter, until Bobby's ears couldn't deal with it.

It was all too much for him.

He watched, as the heat grew and the fever pitch of noise tore all sound from the air. As, in the corner of his eyes, blurred shapes kept swirling, like gravity and sink holes, towards the Reptile, only to burn in plain sight. To fry as the busker moved towards Mona.

But nothing else happened.

The Reptile walked.

The Firebreakers didn't change. None of them breathed fire. There was no power.

I knew it! Bobby thought. *Sassy's friends aren't dragons!*

The Firebreakers just stood there. *Stood there!* Watching three press photographers, cameras at the ready, move in behind the busker.

And while they did nothing, the busker reached for Raglus, grabbed and threw him like rag dolls. Bobby, all beat up and petrified, yelled and yelled, but in the white noise, heard nothing.

Palestine went for his bass, of all things. He tried to play it, but the Reptile slapped him down. There was a mad flurry of camera flashes. The air screamed. Palestine gave a look of pure rage from the floor.

The busker stood over him. Dared him, as more and more flashes went off. As camera shutters open and shut like hailstones. As smoke grew and the air around both of them seemed to burn and die.

Palestine seethed. Yet he kept his eyes on the photographers, stayed on his hands and knees, all human and hurting.

Then Sassy followed his lead and started singing. She bopped, she scat, even though she couldn't be heard, even though she couldn't hear herself. But the words shaped in her lips, her fingers seemed to click. These days she knew what music felt like. Knew its need, its pulse. Its texture.

She knew, like prayer over sandstone cities, that it had a mood. That it started in the heart, not in sound.

And nothing short of death, *nothing*, could take it away from her!

Sassy moved, swayed her head, chin jutting out, as if she was at sorrow-filled peace with the night. And the screaming silence from dark shadows seemed to tint with colours.

The gym seemed to tint with colours.

Of friends and smoky tavern crowds and music.

Bobby held his bleeding head and swollen eye. It was all madness, he was *sure*. Yet his hearing was returning. Just.

'Sis!' he barely heard himself shout.

Then there was a *boom*! The night sky raged at the gym roof, strained and bent at reinforced steel. A storm of lightning, of thunder, of speed and punching winds, thrashed at all things man-made.

Raglus found his trumpet and played with Sassy. Created a mood of jazz and nightclubs that wrestled with the white sound.

There was a click in Bobby's head. His ears returned. He could hear the chaos of storms and fighting.

'Too late!' the busker smiled, as he walked up to Mona.

'You bastard!' Bobby yelled.

'Don't be mad, boy! You're the key!' the Reptile yelled back, as blurred arms seemed to grab, as blurred arms seemed to burn. 'You're a Real Boy! Real World! You don't believe in any of this, do you?'

'No!' Bobby shouted in defiance.

'You don't believe in magic!'

'No!'

'It takes away from real rewards, doesn't it? From the real work and real hardness? From real, arse-kicking victories?'

'Yes!'

'You don't believe in dragons! In hocus-pocus!'

'No!' Bobby raged.

'Or even in Blurs . . .!' the busker laughed, as almost-real things burned. As they clawed free from shadows, to attack the Reptile, only to find the middle of Bobby's unbelieving eyes.

Bobby said nothing. He couldn't just believe when it suited him. He wished he could. He *wished*! But he couldn't. He had no religion. That was his strength. Live while you can. Live good, do good, make your own decisions.

'Keep watching!' the busker smirked, and reached for Mona.

But Bobby knew what he *did* believe in. Loyalty. Family,

strength. In live and let live.

And not in arseholes.

'I don't believe in *you*!' he shouted, with all the gunpowder his lungs could muster.

The busker paused. Everybody, everything, the moment itself, hesitated. For a second, a pathetic, tall, wiry man stood in the middle of a gym with no authority. No presence. None at all.

It was just a second.

But Bobby packed his lack of belief into it and ran. Ran away, as fast as he could.

Ran away to help his sister.

The closer he got to the door, the more he heard weather and drums. Then another *boom*, the echo of thunder. Lights went out all over the neighbourhood. The gym fell to darkness.

'. . . Jodi . . .' said Raglus.

White noise and bad intents became one man's delusions. The press lost their bearings. A wind of blurred, grey shapes rose from the floor, flooding into the hole where Bobby wasn't watching anymore.

'No . . .' the Reptile whispered, as the night consumed him.

The skylight shattered with the weight of something fast and heavy.

Bobby heard the wild thrashing of hateful hands. Juicy, wet, tearing sounds. The clash of flesh and bone. A child's cry.

Then he heard the sloppy thud of something tall and lifeless hitting the floor.

59. Ouch

Two photographers scampered past Bobby into the street. The third paused, built up her courage and made her way back to the gym.

Bobby followed her.

The room was trashed. Dark and silent, with no music or magic in it.

Bobby looked at the bloody body on the gym floor. Even in the dark he could make out the yellow suit, the snare drum at its side. He heard footsteps on broken glass beside him. The whine and pop of a flash.

There was another pop. The press woman was doing her job.

She had been paid to take photos of a midnight fight. Of dragons. Having failed at that, she was taking photos of a body. Her client. The cops, the newspapers, someone would buy them.

When the flash went a third time, Bobby saw the holes in the busker's chest and threw up. But somehow he knew that when the autopsy was done, and more photos were taken, those five finger-like puncture marks would be written up as knife wounds.

Would become knife wounds.

He knew that, if he remembered anything at all, he'd remember being concussed. Confused. Delirious. That he wouldn't remember much.

That he would remember knife wounds.

He felt no danger. No Gathering, no anything. Just nausea.

And glad his sister was away somewhere, lost in music, safe from all this grubbiness.

But Sassy wasn't lost in music.

When the thrashing had stopped, when the hullabaloo had finished, the Firebreakers had turned to see Sassy, lit by moonlight, lying in a pool of blood, unmoving . . .

60. Sweat and Motion

Everything was hazy.

Sassy could feel the sweat on her face, in her clothes, yet the air was cold. She couldn't stop shaking. She was moving. No, something was moving. It was Mona. The singer was carrying her and they were going fast. She felt an incredible sense of motion.

Sassy passed out.

Eventually, Sassy felt wind. Warm wind. She felt weightlessness, could hear the rustle of her clothes, her hair. She tried to open her eyes, but the world was dark and blurry. All she could make out was black. A lot of black. With streaks of tail-light red somewhere below. Darting flashes of dull yellow and traffic lights and neon.

There was a beat.

Steady, strong. Impossibly strong. The wind rose with it, pushed with it. She tried to listen. It sounded like the flap of huge, leather canvasses.

Was she being carried? Flying? Sassy felt scales against her shoulder. Blood that wasn't hers.

She passed out again.

Sassy woke in blurry heat.

Nothing seemed real. She was dizzy, but couldn't raise her head.

There was a cave, a fire. She was sure of it.

Or was it a delirium?

Everything was hot! So hot! Heavy things moved in the shadows around her. Then, through the fog of her eyes, she saw dark green scales, muscles, warm greys. Shapes. Huge shapes, carrying enormous strength. One stopped, towering over her and her blurry vision. It was frightening, mean, hideous, wonderful . . .

'. . . Mona . . .?' Sassy said.

'Hush, child,' the creature growled.

And the heat became too much. Sassy's eyes became too heavy.

'*Fix her!*' she heard the beast roar, as she passed out again.

61. Sound Sucked In

Sassy felt nothing. Not warmth. Not cold. Just nothing.

Nothing.

Time drifted.

She heard leather. The murmur of talk. Its rhythm. She heard nothing. Time drifted.

Sassy felt pain.

Her vision tried to return like rubbish swirls against strong winds. A smudge of shapes were the best her eyes could muster.

'Child,' Mona's voice said. It was beautiful. It was always beautiful.

Sassy tried to speak.

'Shh,' Mona whispered. 'Don't be sad.'

'Sad?'

'Shh. You are glorious.'

'M . . . Mona . . .? I don't . . . Glorious . . .?' Sassy said.

Then her smudged world tuned to black. Sound sucked in, after her vision, and fell and fell and faded.

'. . . hunger . . .' Mona's voice drifted into nothing.

'. . . passion . . .'

62. Jazz, Sorrow and Weather

When Sassy woke, the clock said only forty minutes had passed since the Reptile had hurt her. Yet she felt fine. Rested.

Healthy.

She felt strong, full of strange blood and jazz and weather. She felt confused. She felt numb.

She tried and tried, but just couldn't take in what the doctor was telling her.

'Yes,' he insisted. 'Mona is dead. A life for a life.'

'But . . .'

'Her storm was blowing out. Her passion dying. She was falling the entire time you knew her.'

'Still. I was . . .'

'She was never after an apprentice. She wanted a replacement.'

It all made sense.

That was why Mona didn't help CT Virus. Why she didn't save him by infecting him like she had Sassy. Why she didn't make him something more again, make him not human and dead and dying. That was why the Firebreakers were so desperate to protect Sassy.

A life for a life.

Mona had only one gift to give and she'd already given it.

Sassy didn't have a choice. Not since all that time ago, in her room, in the dark, when Mona had infected her blood with a kiss.

Hallelujah, child . . . she had said. *Hallelujah . . .!*

Sassy tried to shake this numbness from her brain and fingers and heart. But felt nothing.

'I . . . I want to see her . . .' the words fell out.

'Her body's been cremated,' the doctor's voice said. 'Dragons, fire. You know how it is.'

Who is this man talking to me? Sassy thought.

'Who *are* you?' she barked like mad dogs. '*Who are you?!*'

Sassy kicked and thrashed at him as though she was a furious little windmill. But this skinny man was strong.

Stronger than any doctor.

He held her wrists and when she looked at his she could see the vague indent of scales.

'I was a friend of Mona's,' the doctor said. 'Now I'm a friend of yours. You have friends. Not many, but true. You are *music*, Sassy . . .!' he pleaded. 'Just think of it . . .!'

But Sassy was numb. She wasn't thinking anything.

She walked down the doctor's pale white corridor, towards the doors that led to the world, with all its noise and neon and smells and colours. As she did, she noticed things not quite there, in the corner of her eyes. Blurs. Watching over her. Guarding her. Marvelling her.

Sassy didn't care.

She just wanted to get on a boat, before this numbness left her. Go out to sea, where there was an ocean big enough to cry and sing into. An ocean deep enough to take in the fury of sorrow. The wildness of storms.

Her tears for Mona.

63. Invincible

It was a hot morning.

Bobby rapped and tapped out a beat on his jeans. Watched the cars on his way to school. Not all of them, not the shiny, new ones. They all had their windows up, were metallic blue, metallic peach, metallic silver. Airless, rustless, soundless.

The P-plate Turks had that V8 sound. The work vans, the tatty old orange Mazdas, the delivery trucks, they had their windows down. Their exhausts rattled. Bobby walked the main drag an hour after morning peak hour, hoping to get to school some time before recess, taking in people who knew how to drive. Listening to the radios of passing cars with open windows.

A white ute rumbled by, with mud, scars and bog-jobs in every panel. With tools in the back and a song on the tape deck. The sound was rough and raw, terrible. The music muddy. But the driver had one hand out the window taking in the wind, slapping away at his door. His head was bopping, killing time to the song.

Not rockin', not thrashing. Just going with it.

The car drove by. Its tape-deck song spread into open air for two seconds, and went with it.

It was Bobby's song. And Falla's and Johnny's.

He was sure! The 'Walla, walla, walla!' was a dead giveaway.

In all the push and shove, they had left a handful of tapes at the band venue. Anyone could have found one.

Far out, he thought.

Their music was going nowhere, fast. Probably never would. So what? Somewhere out there, for the length of a passing car, for two seconds, his song was a part of the world. As solid as roads. As real as the walls of buildings, as the smell of garbage.

Beyond that, the future just didn't bother him.

Bobby made it to school halfway through English. Everybody sat faces forward, watching Mr Muir, listening to his texta squeak all over the board like a leather-clad go-go dancer.

The teacher didn't once take his eyes off what he was writing.

'And how are you this *afternoon*, Mr Piero?' he drenched his voice in sarcasm.

He was the Enemy.

The world was full of them.

'Sorry, sir,' Bobby held out a late slip. 'My dog died again.'

'Hm . . .' Mr. Muir squeaked away. 'You have a great lot of homework ahead of you, Mr Piero.'

Bobby tapped out a beat. Slapped and tickled his own little something, a sound to match the way car wheels make a sweat, rough rhythm as they glide over gravel. He thought of the white ute. His father, his sister. All the Enemies life had to offer. He thought of no crowds and Ronnie Wicks.

He thought of his music.

'That's okay, sir,' he slapped and tapped. 'I'm invincible.'

64. Searching Echo

Sassy had been gone the longest time. God only knew where.
It worried the hell out of John Piero.

Work had been hard. Damn hard. Yet good money for once.
It was strange. Lately, for some reason, his boss had been looking
after him. Almost scared. It wasn't just the extra money John Piero
liked, hard work didn't bother him. It was a respect thing.

But work was hours ago. Night had come, warm and easy.
Sassy's father sat in a small chair, drifting into sleep. Looking out his
daughter's window.

He listened to Bobby thrashing away, practising with his mates
in a garage down the road. Could picture them, hopeless, belting out
songs to roller doors and brick walls. Charging at the real world.
Loving it, hating it. Attacking it with volume.

There was a knock at the door.

Its sound had an echo that searched the flat in half a second.
The place sounded hollow when the kids weren't there. Hollow
and lonely.

John Piero shuffled, tired, through his lounge, released the lock,
leaving the safety chain on. Through it, he saw a man who wore sweat
like Irish wear freckles.

It was the One Man Carnival.

'Your daughter is playing tonight. Right now,' he said.

'How do you —' John Piero started.

'Down at the docks. She can't come home.'

'So why are —'

'I've been watching you and your family. From the start. She's playing tonight. Can't you tell? There are no Blurs on the street. No ghouls or shadowy shadows. She's at the Blue Duck Hotel down near the drydock, no humans allowed. Then, she is changing, she'll be gone. A long time. You deserve to know.'

'But —'

'I thought you deserve to know, is all.'

John Piero looked at him through the crack in his door. He had so many questions to ask, but didn't. He knew there was no point.

'Thank you,' he said.

The One Man Carnival nodded, as if in agreement of unspoken things.

Then he walked away, with a round man strut, down the corridor, towards the lifts, that connected to the streets, that were missing his volume.

John Piero watched him go.

He went back into Sassy's room to look at the night as he dressed to leave. The heat had built since sunset, he didn't want to wear a jacket.

But a constant, easy rain was falling.

65. Food and Religion

John Piero was wet.

He walked through the Blue Duck's doors. The place had a salty taste, as all good dock bars do. Its crowd wasn't-at-all-right. So many people smoked they all seemed to blur.

John Piero ignored them. Why look? They'd just not be there.

Yet by ignoring them he could see them at last, the things that had been plaguing the corners of his vision.

Many of the Blurs were ugly. These shades, half memories and strange things. Ugly. None of them hid it, none of them cared. Jazz was meant to be full of beautiful people, slick clothes.

Not these creatures, not this crowd.

It wasn't about jazz. It was about music.

And the shadowy people, they loved it. Its flow was as natural as weather, their glue to this earth. Their passion where their hearts had been.

They needed it to survive.

Music was a religion. Air. Food. To them, anyway. It fed them. And to be able to play it, play it well, was to be solid and precious.

John Piero watched his daughter. She sweat under the stagelights, her hair flowed. Her voice slid, controlled and lazy, her eyes stayed closed. She was lost in her own musical world within this lost musical world.

He stood under her, plainly human, blocking the audience's view, but they refused to seethe or boil. He was *her* father. They knew that and deferred to him.

John Piero watched Sassy Piero.

Tears fell. And all the rain in the world couldn't hide them. Would be drowned by them. So didn't try.

John Piero watched his daughter.

And felt proud. Unbelievably proud.

She seemed so on top of it, of everything, even though he knew she wasn't. Not by the length of the sun and the stars. He didn't care how much dodgy time the Firebreakers had taken her through, she was still young. Still naive. Still so small. She had no idea what she was getting into.

But, maybe that was okay.

If people did know how much effort things took, maybe they wouldn't bother to start. Wouldn't commit to paths. They would never have come down from the trees. Wouldn't bother to stage festivals, seal desert roads. To make houses or cities. Cities that needed carpenters, concreters, painters.

That needed plumbers.

They wouldn't take on relationships, or explore atoms, or buy a farm.

Or decide to raise a child.

Sometimes you just had to do, or let someone do. Trust.

Let gravity fall.

Standing under smoky stagelights, juicy orange burning through his brain, John Piero knew he wasn't smart enough to think these thoughts. Not so smoothly. He knew one of these creatures was nudging his mind.

Furious, he tensed and clenched with effort. Tried to force them

out of his head, hard, the way bouncers make sure drunks they evict
land on their faces. He didn't care if he agreed. God damn them.
God damn! His thoughts would be his own!

Then he looked up again.

And saw his daughter's face looking down, through her long
hair, right into his eyes.

She held her microphone stand while Raglus, backed lightly by
Jodi and Palestine, curled and swirled smoky air into a trumpet solo
for the soul. Those thoughts, in his head, were his daughter's. Sassy's.
And he *did* agree with her. And he wasn't furious anymore.

There was so much to be lost about. To doubt over. The only
fact he knew in that moment, and days, weeks and years after it, was
that he didn't own his daughter. That nobody owned their children.
But he had, he hoped, maybe even a little, inspired her to feel.

'I love you,' he said, he worried, with all his dumb plumber's
heart.

He wanted to tell her he was there. Would always be. For comfort
when she was confused, for rage against her enemies, to provide a
strong, stumpy plumber's arm. But he couldn't find the words.

'I know you are,' Sassy smiled, right into his bursting silence.

He watched that smile, her long, sharp teeth, as she tilted her
head up and fell back into song.

Strong, proud, fragile song.

Passionate song.

She was still rough, but her passion fed her timing, became
a presence, a thing felt through the skin as well as heard through
the ears.

She sang her lazy jazz victory to the room. Sang it to smoke and
mysteries and strange things. She tried. She gave food. She
gave moments.

She gave.

Gave through the raw, smooth voice of a child.

The smoke thickened, the stagelights burned rich and warm. There was white, then, slowly, there was red, gradually, there was orange again. The Firebreakers played. Their song shifted. The stage lights shifted with them.

Everything became smoke and deep, rich blue.

Everything blue.

Everything.

The blue of deep sea tides. Of half moons and heartache and love. Blue anger, blue velvet, blue calm. Blue moons. The blue of any and everything that flowed on the dark half of the planet.

The crowd murmured quietly, made little noise.

John Piero tried to look at his daughter, watch her sing, but seemed to lose her in the smoky settings. The harder he tried, the more she would blur, slightly, at the edges.

He wanted to tell her things, so many things. Nothing things. To hug her. But couldn't find her.

He could see it, even though she was performing right in front of him: his daughter was falling away, at speed, into another world.

She was a storm, brewing out at sea. Small and fragile, but with dragons at her side. Living in atmospheres like he lived in time.

She was there. Right there. But going.

Already gone.

Epilogue

Months had passed. Or years. Or weeks. Who knew?

Night was falling.

Sassy looked at the sky. The weather had no idea what it was doing.

She had never taken that boat ride. Had never cried too hard. Not for Mona. Not like she did with desire for music. She didn't know why.

The more Sassy thought about it, the more it bothered her.

Sitting back on Raglus's fire-escape, watching the streetlights and neon mushroom over daylight's fading hour, listening to back window traffic, she let all her questions about her feelings and Mona go. Let their words melt down dry drains, their logic be eaten by traffic.

Kept nothing but their feel. Became simple.

Then, simply, knew their answer.

Sassy walked to the square side of town. Where all the money was. Where most of the jazz was. Where people ate in expensive restaurants and talked and rarely knew and were full of it.

She brought no Firebreakers with her. No instruments. No crew. No baggage.

It had taken her a borrowed night here, a stolen day there. Weeks, all up. Weeks of looking to get this far. It was hard to find something that wasn't special. That left no imprint on shadows. Shadows weren't that hard. They connected to other shadows, covered everything. She felt like a spider at the centre of a web when she was around them.

But shadows hadn't helped. So she had settled for legwork, looking, window after window after window.

And there it was at last. A sight she desperately needed.

Staring through the brown, varnished frame and yellow neon sign of a well-lit restaurant, Sassy saw Mona.

The dark woman wasn't dead.

She was singing jazz. A guitarist was backing her.

Some of the diners listened, some didn't. One or two loved it. Many clapped out of politeness. But, mostly, they ate and talked over her like she was elevator music.

Sassy wanted to tell Mona things. To burst through the door and hug her and spew out amazing tales about the places the Firebreakers had played, the atmospheres they'd set alight, the food they'd fed.

The weather they'd made.

She wanted to run like water downhill to Mona and tell her about the wild music, the churning hunger, the awkward notes, the passion. To *sing* to her about the passion! To sing *with* her! She had the words, could explain anything, when she sang.

But Sassy stopped herself. Looked more.

Mona had nothing special about her, carried no magic in her timing, seemed less cool and more bored. She was okay, but the flame wasn't there. She was old. Way old. Human.

Some humans had the flame, but Mona wasn't one of them. She had given a life for a life, just like the doctor had said. But *he* had healed Sassy's body, with medical knowledge and tricks of time. The life Mona had given her was of magic.

Now Mona was dead to it, like CT Virus before her. Trapped by time. By age and creeping death. Living within the gravity of the Green Mile.

The Yearning.

And, out in the night, hidden by brown woodwork and yellow neon, surrounded by headlights and tail-lights and traffic lights, Sassy remembered CT Virus and the horrible pain reminders gave him.

She loved Mona with all her heart for giving her the platform for her passion. Loved the jazz singer too much to hurt her.

'Thank you,' she whispered to the window, and moved on.

And the One Man Carnival, standing unnoticed behind her, watching, guarding, for once, didn't have to say anything.